PUFFIN  CLASSICS

Awake and Dreaming

D1385183

KIT PEARSON

Awake and Dreaming

INTRODUCED BY
KENNETH OPPEL

PUFFIN

an imprint of Penguin Random House Canada Young Readers,
a Penguin Random House Company

First published in Viking hardcover by Penguin Canada Books Inc., 1996
Published in Puffin paperback by Penguin Canada Books Inc., 1998, 2007
Published in this edition, 2013

2 3 4 5 6 7 8 9 10 (FRI)

Manufactured in Canada.

ISBN 978-0-14-318788-2 (pbk.)

www.penguinrandomhouse.ca

Penguin
Random House
PUFFIN CANADA

For
Marit and Charlotte Mitchell,
Anne Barringer
and
Will Pearson,
who all contributed

Was it a vision, or a waking dream?
Fled is that music:—Do I wake or sleep?

– *JOHN KEATS*

INTRODUCTION BY
KENNETH OPPEL

When I was a kid, I wanted all sorts of things: a tree house, a dog, a spaceship like the Millennium Falcon, a set of friends like the ones I read about in my favourite books. What Theo longs for in *Awake and Dreaming* is a better family. She has no siblings, she's poor, and her single mom is hopeless. Theo doesn't even have the same bedroom or school for very long because she moves around so much. When she wakes up one day as part of a perfect family, it seems too good to be true.

This is one my favourite books, which you might think is weird since the stories I write are usually filled with peril and gruelling quests and heroics. But *Awake and Dreaming* is filled with these same ingredients. This is not a "quiet" book. It is noisy with the most important kinds of struggle, because you and I face them every day: the quest to find our place in the world, to belong to a family and group of friends, to be loved. So I consider this book a page-turner of the best kind.

There are very few writers who can capture the life of an imaginative young person as well as Kit Pearson. Theo is a great character: bookish, shy, wary, brimming with dreams, stubborn, and surprisingly strong. She treasures her "shining moments" just like another great character, Emily of New Moon, who sometimes has "the flash" of perfect happiness. Despite her many strengths, Theo is not perfect. Like everyone, she makes mistakes and has shortcomings, including rejecting overtures of friendship—one of the things she most craves. But what's amazing is that, reading the book, you'll feel like you know her completely; you may even feel you're a lot like her.

When Theo almost magically becomes part of the Kaldor family, it's a dream come true. She now has two brothers and two sisters, all interesting and wonderful. She has amazing, loving parents. She starts at a great new school. But this isn't the end of the story; it's only the beginning. As a reader, you'll be incredibly happy that Theo's found this perfect family and devastated when she loses it. But then the book gets even more interesting because Theo has to learn to accept and embrace the life she has, with all its many imperfections.

On this most gruelling of quests, she gets help from places both expected and unexpected: from her dull but responsible Aunt Sharon, her immature and unreliable mother, and even from a ghost. For a dreamer like

Theo, it's hard to settle for second best when you've had a glimpse of perfection. But this is where her love of books comes in handy. Like any smart reader, she eventually realizes that the perfect life of the Kaldors, while comforting, would make very poor story material. It lacks drama and struggle. And it's these very things, the things Theo wants most to avoid, that will make her real life—and this story—all the richer and more rewarding.

This is an amazingly profound realization, whether you're nine or ninety, and it's a testament of Pearson's skill as a writer that she manages to convey it so naturally to young readers. There's no preachiness here, or sentimentality. Theo learns from experience.

It's impossible not to be completely absorbed in the world of *Awake and Dreaming*. I find it just as gripping and heart-wrenching every time I read it. It certainly counts as a "shining moment" in my reading life.

PROLOGUE

The ghost was restless.

All day she'd watched the visitors to the cemetery—joggers, bundled-up families pushing strollers, couples having earnest conversations. Many of the visitors were on Sunday walks but others had come to visit the graves of relatives. Beside the ghost a family stood around a grassy plot, shivering in the chilly air. They spoke in solemn voices and left some flowers in a tin.

"They'll be wilted in a day," muttered the ghost.

She watched a young man trim a holly bush in front of a marble tablet. He came every Sunday to visit his mother's grave. A growing shrub *lasts*, the ghost thought approvingly.

No one had ever left anything on her grave—not a single flower. On this dank January day her plot looked especially dreary, blanketed with the dead leaves that had lain there all winter.

The ghost strode along the path overlooking the sea, then sat on a step of the war memorial to watch the sun set. All the Sunday visitors had left. Crows circled the empty cemetery, reclaiming it with jeering cries. The wind rose and bare tree branches scraped against one another. Below the ghost, across the road, tumultuous waves flung pebbles on the shore. The full moon seemed to sway in the sky like a lantern.

The ghost smiled. It's a *spooky* night, she thought. A good setting for a ghost story … She always felt less lonely when she was by herself, away from people who reminded her that she was no longer one of them.

Finally it was late enough to go into the house.

SHE NEVER VISITED her former home until its inhabitants were asleep. She'd never had any evidence that people could see her; but maybe they'd hear her or somehow sense her presence if she were there in the daytime. And she didn't want to frighten anyone; she knew she hadn't been left here for that.

Her house wasn't far away—just across the street. The ghost melted into the wood of the door and passed through to the other side. Pausing in the hall, she listened to the hum of the refrigerator and the gurgle of the aquarium. Everyone—all the children and their parents—seemed to be asleep.

Then the family dog ambled out from the kitchen. But

he was used to her nightly visits; he thumped his tail and went sleepily back to his cushion.

The ghost went into a room lined with books. The familiar space comforted her—she'd known it all her life. Of course this house didn't belong to her any more. It hadn't for forty years. But she had been born here; this was where she had suffered and triumphed and dreamed.

She scanned the bookshelves and picked out a Trollope novel she'd never got around to reading. Settling into an armchair, she sighed with relief as the book drew her in.

She didn't look up until just before dawn. For the past few hours she'd managed to forget her frustration and loneliness, or even if she were alive or dead. She had been sealed in the story, as caught in the author's spell as she'd been as a child.

She leaned back and closed her eyes. Another chair had once stood in this same spot—a chair with a tall back and winged sides, where a child could curl herself small and be almost invisible …

SHE IS NINE YEARS OLD, sitting in that chair—her favourite chair, where she escapes to read. It's Saturday afternoon. Father is at his club. Mother has Mrs. Currie and Mrs. Roberts over for lunch. The child can hear the clink of cups and spoons in the dining-room.

She is supposed to be having a rest after her own lunch in the kitchen. But she came downstairs to look for a new book and retreated to the wing chair after she'd found one on her special shelf.

The book is called *The Princess and the Goblin*. The child sniffs its leather cover and reverently unfolds it. She carefully turns the crackly pages to the first enticing words: "There was once a little princess whose father was king over a great country full of mountains and valleys."

Unfastening the tight straps on her shoes, she lifts her feet onto the chair and props the book on her knees. With a happy sigh she falls into Princess Irene's world.

The child is reading so intently she barely hears the hum of voices near her. At first they seem like voices on the other side of a wall—the wall of the story she's engrossed in. But suddenly she realizes the voices are right in the room. She freezes.

Mother will be angry that she's in the study instead of upstairs. But the chair faces the window, its high back a barricade to the three women chatting near the door. If she is extremely still they might not detect her.

"Here it is," Mother says. "I knew I'd put it in this drawer. There you are, Muriel. I think you'll agree it's the best seed catalogue."

"Thank you for lending it to me, Philippa," she hears Mrs. Currie say.

"That was a delicious lunch," says Mrs. Roberts. "We got a lot planned for the next garden meeting, didn't we? Next month it's my turn."

They go on with thank-yous and goodbyes, but no one moves from the study. The child squirms, trying not to let a leg show. Mother's friends always take so long to say goodbye—why can't they just *leave*?

"What a gloomy room this is," sighs Mother. She walks over and pulls one of the heavy curtains open a little farther. The child's heart thuds so strongly she's sure Mother can hear it; but nothing happens.

"I think it's a pleasant room," says Mrs. Roberts politely. "All these books! What a reader Giles must be."

"He treats this room like his private kingdom," says Mother. "He won't let me decorate it and he complains if the maid moves anything." She sighs again. "And now my only child is becoming just like him. Every time I complain that she reads too much, Giles tells me to let her be. He's filled a special shelf with books for her and he's always adding to them."

"How is the dear child?" asks Mrs. Currie. "I haven't seen her since our Wendy's birthday party." She suppresses a giggle. "I'm sorry, Philippa, I didn't mean to laugh."

"It's quite all right," says Mother. "It was rather funny, wasn't it?" But her voice is not amused. "Walking right into a pond in her best clothes! Daydreaming, as usual. Now she refuses to go to any parties."

The child blushes as hotly as she did when they fished her out of the garden pond, strings of green slime hanging from her hair and her white dress.

She *had* been daydreaming. She'd been pretending she was a queen, to keep from crying when the girls called her "Horseface," as they did every day in school. When she'd followed the other children into the house for birthday cake, she had been leading an imaginary royal procession—and fallen into the pond without seeing it. She could still hear the girls' jeering laughter as she'd splashed and spluttered.

Mother's voice sounds desperate. "I'm at my wit's end about her. All she wants to do is read—or she wanders in the cemetery for hours and comes back looking more like a rough little boy than a girl. Sometimes she just stares into space, as if she's in a trance. I've tried to ask other children over, but she seems to want to be alone. And it doesn't help that she's as plain as a boot on top of it. I really don't know what to do with her. And Giles is no help. Apart from encouraging her to read, he seems to barely notice her."

"She'll get over it," says Mrs. Currie.

"It's just a phase," adds Mrs. Roberts. "My niece was a loner too—until she turned fifteen. Then she noticed young men and now she's happily married with two babies. Don't worry about her, Philippa."

"I try not to," says Mother.

"We really *must* be going," says Mrs. Roberts. The voices fade into the hall.

The child stays in her frozen position until the

goodbyes are finally over and Mother's footsteps go back to the dining-room. Then she releases a huge breath, as if she's expelling all the words she's heard. She looks down and lets the book take her away.

THE BRIGHTENING DAWN roused the ghost from her memories. She stood up, her book sliding to the floor. It was time to go.

After she left the house, she paused at the entrance to the cemetery, watching the early sun glint on the wet grass.

Reading had been a welcome escape from her restlessness, but now she paced in despair. When was she going to find what she'd spent the last forty years searching for?

The ghost turned away from the cemetery. What she yearned for—the reason she was compelled to linger in this world—wasn't in there. It was time to do some more travelling.

PART 1

Theo

1

Across the strait, in a larger city on the same sea, another child sat as still as the long-ago child in the study.

The grade-four classroom thrummed with activity. Chairs screeched against the floor and high voices bossed and giggled. Pens and scissors clattered on desktops as the students drew and cut out and scribbled for their coastal forest projects.

Theo was as fixed in the middle as a rock. Waves of chatter rose and fell around her. The other three in her group—Robert and Yogita and Jason—made no attempt to involve her. When Mr. Barker had told her to push over her desk and join them, Yogita had held her nose and smirked. Now she and the others reached in front of Theo and argued over who would write about spotted owls as if she were invisible.

Theo held a book about trees open on her lap. But her eyes stared blankly as she retreated into her daydream.

She was thinking about magic. Last night she'd finished a wonderful book called *Five Children and It*. The story was about some kids who found a strange creature called a Psammead that granted wishes. There were four older children—Cyril, Anthea, Robert and Jane—and a baby brother. Theo liked Anthea the best. She seemed about eleven; Jane was probably nine, like Theo. Most of the wishes had backfired. They had wished to be beautiful—but then no one had recognized them.

I wouldn't wish for *that*, thought Theo, I'd wish for—

"Hey, Licehead!" Robert jabbed her side with his ruler. "Didn't you hear the bell?"

Theo blinked. The other kids were thundering out of the classroom for recess. She stood up slowly, forcing herself to come back.

Robert was hunting for something in his desk. He looked up. "Why do you always stare into space like that? What are you thinking about?"

Now he sounded more curious than mean. But Theo rubbed the place his ruler had poked. The Robert in the book wouldn't have hurt her.

She noticed how Robert's red hair stood up on his forehead. You look like a rooster, she decided. A stupid, show-offy rooster.

Robert backed away as Theo kept staring at him. "So don't answer," he said from the doorway. "Who cares? Nobody cares about you, Licehead."

"How ARE YOU getting along, Theo?" Mr. Barker asked her after recess. Theo had already learned to linger by the outside door and come up to the classroom first, before she got trapped in a jeering group.

The teacher's voice was kind, but Theo shrank from the hand he put on her shoulder. "Fine," she whispered.

"It's hard to start at a new school, especially in January," said Mr. Barker. Loud voices and footsteps advanced down the hall. "Are you making friends?"

Theo couldn't answer such a dumb question. Hadn't he noticed that she was always alone?

"I know it takes time. But you'll soon feel at home." Chubby Mr. Barker was as relentlessly positive as a bouncing ball. The other kids called him a pushover. They often persuaded him to have a video instead of arithmetic.

Theo sat down with relief. Across the aisle Nita smiled. Theo lowered her head.

Nita had been assigned to take care of her on her first day at this school last week. She was kind. Crystal and Meiko were kind too. But they wore different clothes every day and the right kind of shoes. Theo was sure their kindness was just an act for the teacher.

In her previous school she hadn't known this. Kyla, too, had worn clean clothes and included Theo in her conversations. She was pretty and funny and for a few weeks Theo had been flattered that Kyla had chosen her as a friend. But then she'd been the only girl in the class not invited to Kyla's birthday party.

This was the second of the five schools Theo had attended where there was a mixture of well-off kids and poor kids. Now she knew you couldn't trust the well-off kids.

And the poor kids were too much like herself. The first day it was hard to pick them out; wearing sloppy clothes was the style and everyone looked the same. But now she knew the kids who, like her, had dirty hair and wore the same clothes for a week. They were either tough or as quiet and wary as she was.

At least Theo wasn't the only person in the room who was called "Licehead." If she made friends with Angela or Jennifer or Kandice, perhaps the name wouldn't sting as much. But that would be admitting she was like them— poor and inferior, the type of person who was called names.

None of the kids in her schools were as interesting as kids in books.

The long day dragged on. Theo dully guessed at the answers in her arithmetic book and pretended to listen to an earnest woman talk to them about constructive ways to express anger. At lunch she sat alone, chewing slowly on her dry jam sandwich to make it last longer.

That was a major problem with this school. Like the last one, there was no hot-breakfast program. Two schools ago there'd even been a free lunch. Theo tried not to think of hamburgers or hot dogs or to gaze too obviously at the boy beside her, who was devouring a large piece of chocolate cake.

After lunch Mr. Barker tried to get them to write poetry. Theo was thinking so intently about the Psammead that she didn't hear a thing he said.

Then he was standing over her. "Theo? Do you understand what I want you to do?" He smiled. "Just choose one of the lines on the board and make up a poem about it. It doesn't even have to rhyme! You can write it any way you like!" He seemed to burst with goodwill, as if he were giving her a present.

Theo blinked at him, and nodded. A poem … She looked at the board.

What is pink? (or choose some other colour)
What is peace?
What is love?
What is friendship?
What is happiness?

She looked around—everyone else was already scribbling. She began to write slowly.

After twenty minutes Mr. Barker clapped his hands. "All right, people! Let's have some volunteers to read their poems."

No one raised a hand. "How about you, Nita?" asked the teacher, smiling.

"It's not very good."

"I'm sure it's *wonderful*! Don't forget, we're all *writers* here! Let's hear what you've created. Stand up and use a good loud voice."

Nita stood up and mumbled, "'What is happiness? Happiness is a warm puppy. Happiness is opening Christmas presents. Happiness is your mum and dad kissing you good night.' That's as far as I got."

"*Excellent*, Nita!" beamed Mr. Barker. "You really tried to express your feelings!"

"I don't think it's very good," said Robert. "She didn't make it all up herself. I've heard that part about a warm puppy before."

"Well, sometimes poets echo other poets—but not on purpose, eh, Nita?"

Nita glared at Robert.

"How about you, Robert?" asked Mr. Barker.

"Sure!" Robert jumped to his feet. "'What is peace? Peace is when there's no more war. What is war? War is shooting and guns and bombs. What are bombs? Bombs are—'"

"That's enough, Robert," said Mr. Barker. "I think we get the idea." For a second he almost frowned, but then his expression became even jollier. "Good for you! It was very creative of you to extend the original premise like that!"

"It's an *awful* poem!" said Nita. "It's way too violent."

"It's how Robert feels … what he *wanted* to write. That's the most important thing," said Mr. Barker. "Now, who wants to be next?"

After Lindsay read her long poem about love and Adam his rhymed couplets about peace, Mr. Barker became more and more excited as he searched for extravagant words of praise for each of them.

"Now let's see … How about … Theo!"

Theo jerked to attention. She'd been looking out the window and imagining what it would be like to be able to leap from tree to tree like a squirrel. "What?"

"How would you like to read us your poem?"

"No, thank you."

"Well, then … how about if *I* read it?"

Theo shrugged; she knew she didn't have a choice. Mr. Barker took the paper off her desk.

"'What is grey? Grey is cold rain. Grey is a scratchy blanket. Grey is a hard sidewalk. Grey is a rat in the bin. Grey is no colour at all.'"

There was silence. In front of Theo, Angela turned around and gave her an understanding look.

"A *rat*!" said Yogita finally. "Yeck!"

"That's too depressing for a poem," said Shannon. "Poems are supposed to be happy, like Nita's."

Mr. Barker seemed to be swelling like a balloon. Then his words spewed out all at once. "I think it's *brilliant*!

Superb! It's original and evocative and full of emotion! Poems *don't* have to be happy, Shannon. I'm delighted Theo reminded us of that." He put the paper back on Theo's desk, practically jumping up and down with enthusiasm. "*Very* well done, Theo! Excellent!"

For a second Theo felt a tinge of pride. Mr. Barker really seemed to like her poem.

But he'd acted excited about the others, too. He was obviously just trying to be nice to her.

At last the closing bell went and school was over for the day. Theo rushed out of the room.

THE SCHOOL LIBRARY was crammed into a space that was much too small for it. Books and magazines and computers lined every surface. There was barely enough room to walk between the shelves and tables and bean-bag chairs. The librarian, Ms. Cohen, wasn't there, but students were allowed to check books in and out on their own. Theo took *Five Children and It* from her bag and signed it in. Then she went over to the fiction section.

Choosing a new book was like looking for treasure. Theo always took a good long time. First she examined some paperbacks on a revolving stand. But they were mostly novels about one girl or one boy with a problem, or horror stories with scary covers. That wasn't what she wanted.

She knew she'd have better luck on the shelves where the older hardcover books were kept. She walked along looking at them slowly, tilting her head to read the titles. *Half Magic, The Moffats, The Family from One End Street* ... Theo tingled with pleasure as she recognized favourites from other libraries.

At her last school there had been only paperbacks. But this new library was the best kind—it didn't throw out its old books. They looked ugly, with their thick, plain covers. But the dull outsides concealed the best stories.

Usually a title would leap out at her, as if it were shouting, "Read *me*!" And here it was—*All-of-a-Kind Family*. Theo pulled it off the shelf. The cover was sturdy and green, with a faded picture on it. It showed five girls in matching old-fashioned dresses and pinafores tumbling down some stairs. They were all smiling and, best of all, they were holding books!

Theo opened it up, read the enticing first sentence, then sighed with relief. She'd found the right book.

Ms. Cohen was back at her desk when Theo returned to it. She smiled. "Hello, there! Theo Caffrey, isn't it?"

Theo nodded.

"Is Theo short for something?"

"Theodora," mumbled Theo.

"That's a beautiful name. What have you found today? Oh, you'll love this. I read it when I was your age! What a lot of books you've taken out in only a week! You're an exceptional reader for your age. Why don't you pick some more? You can take as many as you like."

"No, thank you," said Theo. Ever since she'd lost a library book and Rae had had to pay for it, she wouldn't let Theo take home more than one book at a time.

"Well, enjoy it. It's a treat to see these wonderful old stories being borrowed." The librarian checked out the book, handed it back, and gazed at Theo thirstily. "I just wish some of the others read as many good books as you do."

Theo flushed and put the book into her bag. Librarians always went into ecstasy over her. Soon she'd be called in to the counsellor to find out why she did so poorly in school, in spite of the fact that she read so much.

BEHIND THE SCHOOL was a grassy playground. Even though it was raining, Theo sat down on a swing, watching the water dribble down the shiny wood of the teeter-totters. She swayed gently, pretending she was a princess.

This is the royal park, she thought. Over there are peacocks and fountains. In a few minutes I will be called in to dinner by my nanny and eat roast chicken and mashed potatoes off golden plates …

"Hi, Theo!" Theo looked up and tried to focus. It was Angela, holding hands with a tired-looking woman in a shapeless black coat. "Mum, this is Theo, a new girl in our class."

Angela's mother smiled, but she didn't seem to speak English.

"I really liked your poem," said Angela shyly. "I thought it was the best in the class! It sounded so—so *real*."

"Mmm," said Princess Theo haughtily. She willed Angela to go away so she could continue her game.

Angela's eager smile turned to disappointment. "Well, goodbye. See you tomorrow." She led her mother away and Theo immediately forgot about them.

She tried to carry on being a princess but her pants were soaked and it was getting late.

She began to walk home. Her wet hair dripped into her eyes and water seeped through the cracked soles of her runners. Her toes bumped painfully against the fronts.

Theo always lingered on the first part of the walk, where renovated old houses were crowded together pleasantly. She stopped in front of her favourite house. Its blue window boxes were planted with tiny fir trees that were still decorated with red bows for Christmas. The front door was sunny yellow. It looked like a house in a little child's drawing—bright and friendly and neat. On the top floor was a small round window like a peep-hole. That would be my room, thought Theo.

After she passed the hospital, the houses became shabbier; then they were replaced by low apartment buildings. The closer Theo came to her own block, the louder the traffic noise from the busy street behind it.

Theo stopped at the corner store beside her apartment. She stooped to pick up two cigarette butts for Rae. Then she slinked into the store, hoping the owner had a customer. But he was alone and kept his eyes on her as she examined the candy display.

The longer she looked, the more moist her mouth became. Two days ago she'd managed to sneak a chocolate bar into her pocket when the store owner was helping someone.

The week before Rae was paid was always a lean one. All Theo had had to eat today were two jam sandwiches—one for breakfast and one for lunch.

"Are you going to buy anything or not?" the man growled.

Theo shook her head and scuttered out of the store. She couldn't put off going home any longer.

2

The lobby of the small grey building smelled like cabbage. Theo trudged down the dingy stairwell and along the hall of the basement, pushing past someone's laundry hung to dry. A TV game show blared from behind Mrs. Mitic's door.

Opening her own door, Theo took out the cigarette butts, then dropped her sodden jacket. She pried off her wet shoes and socks and rubbed her sore toes. The same show droned from the small TV in the living-room.

"*Where* have you been?" scolded Rae. She stood up. "It's almost four-thirty! You know I have to be out of here in an hour."

"Sorry," mumbled Theo.

Her mother began stirring something on the stove. Theo dropped the cigarette butts into an overflowing ashtray on the table.

"It takes me half an hour longer to get to work from this place," complained Rae, as she dished out Kraft

Dinner for each of them. "I told that to Derek yesterday when I was late and do you know what he said? 'Too bad, you'll just have to leave earlier.' Doesn't he think I do? It's the damn bus that's never on time, but he doesn't believe me. And he nagged at me again for not wearing a hair net. And then he wouldn't help Leona and me when this drunk guy called us 'babes.' He just laughed! One of these days I'm going to tell Derek exactly what I think of him. He pisses me off so much! Theo? Are you listening?"

Theo had been cramming macaroni and cheese into her mouth so fast she'd burned her tongue. She took a long drink of water from her glass. The game show had ended and now the canned laughter of a comedy filled the room.

"You never listen!" said Rae. "Look at me, I have something to tell you."

Theo tried to pay attention as Rae lit a cigarette and blew a cloud of smoke over the table. Her mother was beautiful. She had long rippling blonde hair, a perfect nose and blue-green eyes. But there were always etched circles under her eyes from working the late shift at the restaurant, and although she was only twenty-five her skin was lined like that of a much older woman.

"I don't want you to go to school tomorrow," said Rae.

"Why?"

"We're going downtown to do some panning."

"Oh, no, Rae! I hate that!"

"I'm sorry, but we have to. Our money's almost gone and yesterday I got no tips."

"I have an important test tomorrow," Theo tried saying.

"Huh! Since when have you cared about tests? You can write it the next day—I'll give you a note saying you were sick."

"But—" Theo stopped as she watched anger flicker on Rae's face. Sometimes Rae slapped.

"That's settled, then," said her mother. "So, kid, do you think I should put a red rinse in my hair? Donna did and it looks great!"

Theo shrugged. But now that Rae was in a good mood again, she ventured a request.

"Rae, I really need shoes. These ones are too small and they leak."

"But I just got them for you in November!"

"They were already worn out. I guess my feet have grown again." Theo wished they would stop. Shoes were a constant worry.

"Well, maybe on my day off I'll take you to the Sally Ann."

Theo took a deep breath. "Do you think—do you think we could afford new ones? I saw some purple slip-ons in the drug store. They were only ten dollars."

"If they were only ten dollars, they won't last any longer than used ones."

Theo looked so downcast that Rae said, "Cheer up, Kitten. I'll tell you what. If we make a lot of money tomorrow I'll take you to Metrotown and buy you some shoes in a real shoe store, okay?" She was using her sweet look-what-a-good-mother-I-am voice. Theo hated that voice—especially since Rae believed it.

And it wouldn't happen. They wouldn't make enough money, and whatever they did make would be used for food and cigarettes.

Hours later Theo huddled in bed, clutching a thin grey blanket around her shoulders. But she didn't feel the cold. She was away—deep in the ending of *All-of-a-Kind Family*, as the five girls revelled in their new baby brother. She finished the last words and pored over the picture of them all going for a walk. Then she closed the book softly and lay down.

What a wonderful family! They were poor, like her, but they didn't seem so; they were rich with love and laughter. What would it be like to belong to them? Which one would she want to be? Maybe Henny …

Now Theo began to shiver. This apartment was draftier than the last one and the landlord controlled the heat. She got out of bed, put on socks, a tuque and a sweatshirt, then laid her coat and a small rug on top of the blanket. She crept under it all carefully and squeezed herself into a ball.

The evening was the best part of the day, after Rae had gone to work and Theo was left alone with her book. Mrs. Mitic was supposed to look in on her, but she never did; she was too absorbed in her television.

Rae always wanted Theo to watch TV with her when she was home, but Theo turned if off as soon as her mother left for work. She would read every evening until her book was finished, or until her eyes felt so gritty she had to stop and go to sleep.

Theo had found out about books two years ago. Rae only read the magazines that restaurant cutomers left behind, and she had never read to Theo.

But Theo had a faint memory of sitting on someone's knee, looking at pictures of Peter Rabbit and Wild Things and a cat called Zoom while a kind voice told her about them. That must have been at her grandmother's house in Victoria, before she turned three and went to live with Rae in Vancouver.

After that there were no more stories for years. But in grade two, after she'd learned to read, Theo had picked up a book called *Charlotte's Web* in her classroom. She began it in free reading time, carried on secretly on her lap behind her desk, and finished it after she'd sneaked it home. She and Rae were in between apartments then, living at a shelter.

Theo had sat in a corner away from the other kids. She wept inside herself as the brave spider said goodbye and died. Those days immersed in *Charlotte's Web* were like living in a brightly lit, safe room, like the fragrant warm barn where Charlotte and Wilbur lived.

From then on Theo escaped to that bright world whenever she could. Each of her schools had a library. At first Theo read the first book she grabbed from the shelf. She devoured picture books about George and Martha, chapter books about freckle juice and fried worms, and facts about building igloos and about faraway countries like India. Then one day she picked up *Thumbelina* and for a whole year she read nothing but fairy tales— thin and fat volumes about Cinderella and the Sleeping Beauty and the Seven Swans.

Now her favourites were stories about families or stories about magic. Perfect books combined both, like the Narnia chronicles about four children who visited a magic land, or *Half Magic*, where a family found a coin that granted them half of each wish.

Theo knew the families in these books as well as if they were her own sisters and brothers. Meg, Jo, Beth and Amy in Little Women, Pauline, Petrova and Posy in *Ballet Shoes*, John, Susan, Titty and Roger in the "Swallows and Amazons" series …

Outside the window a siren wailed. Someone smashed a bottle and a man's voice cursed. This was the scariest time of Theo's evenings alone. After she finished reading, she couldn't help thinking that someone might climb in the window, or that the rustling noises in the kitchen weren't mice, but some kind of monster under the sink. Even if she had to pee, she couldn't make herself get up this late; what if something was waiting in the bathroom to grab her? Sometimes she would wet the bed and Rae would yell at her in the morning.

If only Calico Cat were curled up on the end of her bed. Calico Cat had really belonged to the man down the hall in their last apartment. But many evenings she had come in Theo's window and visited her, her elegant body twisting around Theo's feet and purring. But when the landlord had raised the rent, they had had to leave that apartment, as they'd left so many. Did Calico Cat miss her? wondered Theo.

She clutched her old doll. Sabrina's hair stood up in matted tufts all over her balding head. Her dirty rubber body smelled and she had a hole in one arm, carefully patched with a bandage. Her dress had once been pink but was now a stained grey.

But her blue eyes still opened and shut. Theo had had her for as long as she could remember. "It's all right, Sabrina," she whispered. "Don't be scared."

If she lay very still, she could usually escape into her going-to-sleep vision—what she would do if someone granted her a wish. If there really was magic, like a Psammead or a magic coin, Theo knew exactly what she'd wish for …

There would be four children, two boys and two girls. She would be the fifth, cozily in the middle with an older brother and sister to protect her, and younger ones to play with. There would a calm mother and father who never yelled or hit or complained to her. They would all live in a big warm house with lots of food, and new shoes whenever you needed them, and hundreds of books, and a cat …

Magic … that was what she needed. If only she had magic, Theo would wish for a family.

3

She sat beside her mother on the bus. At least it had stopped raining. And as much as she hated panning, it wasn't as bad as binning—patrolling the lanes and fishing returnable bottles and other objects out of garbage bins. Theo shivered, trying not to think of the rats they sometimes surprised.

As the bus whined over the bridge to downtown, she gazed at the mountains that rose behind the skyscrapers. They looked so close. What if the bus kept going to the North Shore and climbed right to the top of that mountain? They would get out in dazzling snow. Maybe a different kind of people lived there, who looked like trolls. Maybe they would ask Theo …

"Theo, stop daydreaming! This is our stop!" Rae pulled her off the bus.

The stores had just opened and only a few people were outside. Theo stuck close to Rae as they walked down Granville Street looking for the best spot. In some of the doorways sleeping bodies were rolled up in blankets.

Rae picked a place on the sunny side of the street, in front of a service door between two theatres. She spread out the grey blanket from Theo's bed and set up a portable tape recorder on it. In front of it she placed a shallow cardboard box holding a few coins. Then she sat down on the blanket and lit a cigarette. She got out the sign saying "We Are Hungry" and leaned it against her knees.

"Take off your jacket," she told Theo.

"Can't I wait a while? There's no one around, and it's cold."

"A bunch of people just got off that bus. Please, Theo … you'll warm up after you start."

Theo took off her jacket. Underneath was a short frilly dress that pulled under the armpits—she'd had it for three years. Her legs were wrapped in grubby white tights and she wore her only shoes, the cracked runners. She hugged her chest as she waited for Rae to switch on the tape recorder.

"Okay, kid. Go to it."

As the familiar opening to the Nutcracker began, Theo started to dance. She jumped around awkwardly in a kind of jig.

More people began to fill up the sidewalk, but no one put any coins in the box.

"Smile!" said Rae, as the relentless tune continued. A

woman and child came out of the fast-food restaurant on the corner. They stopped in front of them. Theo tried to smile and examine them at the same time. The girl was about her age, dressed in a red duffel coat and a bright blue beret. She gaped at Theo as if she were from another planet.

"Poor little thing," said the girl's mother. She opened her purse. "Here, Caitlin, give her this."

The girl advanced gingerly, dropped a ten-dollar bill into the box, ran back to her mother and took her hand.

"Doesn't she make you feel lucky?" said the woman as they walked away. Caitlin glanced back over her shoulder. She looked scared.

Theo wondered why she wasn't in school at this time of day. Maybe she was on the way to the dentist's and was having a treat first—kids did that in books. Theo hadn't been to a dentist since the last time they were on welfare, two years ago.

"Ten dollars!" said Rae. "What a great start!" The tape had ended and she flipped it over.

"Can't I rest?" asked Theo.

"After this side. We can't stop while we're having so much luck."

The music on the second side was slower: selections from *Swan Lake*. Theo made vague, ballet-like movements with her arms and legs and tried to pretend she was Posy from *Ballet Shoes*. Several more passersby stopped and dropped some change into the box. They acted either mushy or embarrassed. No one else left any bills.

Theo hated the way they stared at her as if she were a performing animal. When she'd been four and five she hadn't minded as much. She'd skipped around and they'd received more money. Now Rae had to keep reminding her to lift up her feet and smile.

At last she was allowed to have a break. She and Rae huddled on the blanket and took turns sipping tea out of the Thermos Rae had brought. They kept the music on and a few people still dropped coins in the box. "Look sad," whispered Rae. That was easier than trying to smile.

THEY KEPT AT IT for three hours. More and more people filled up the sidewalks and the air became warmer. Vendors set up jewellery stands which sparkled in the sun. A few other panhandlers appeared. One played a violin so well that Theo wished they could shut off their tinny music and just listen. A tattered man sat bleakly a few yards away, hardly looking up when someone dropped money in his hat. Buses screeched and steamed up and down the street and couriers on fast bikes zoomed by.

The pile of change in the box was growing. They were having such a lucky day that Rae wouldn't let Theo rest much. The soles of her feet stung and she felt dizzy.

"How dare you!" A tall, sleek woman in a navy blue suit

was standing in front of them. Theo stopped dancing. The woman was glaring at Rae.

"How can you exploit your own child like that? Can't you see she's exhausted? You people make me sick. Why don't you get a job?"

Rae jumped up and hurled such a strong volley of swear words at the woman that she backed up. She turned and walked quickly away.

"What nerve!" Rae was clenching her fists and breathing hard. "It's none of her business! You're my child, not hers!"

She looked at Theo and her expression became even angrier. "Sit *down*! Why didn't you *tell* me you were tired?" Theo collapsed on the blanket and her mother switched off the tape recorder. "I can't stand this stupid music any longer!"

She leaned against the door and closed her eyes. Cautiously, Theo moved back and joined her.

The violinist had moved on. Pigeons strutted up and down the sidewalk. Theo could smell hot oil from the restaurant. Her stomach gurgled and she wondered what they were going to do for lunch. But Rae kept perfectly still with her eyes closed. Was she still angry? Was she asleep? Then Theo noticed that tears were sliding out from her lowered lids.

"Rae? Are you all right?"

Rae opened her eyes, flicked the tears away and lit a

cigarette. "Oh, Kitten … what kind of life is this?" Her voice was broken. "Look at us! Two *beggars* …"

"We made a lot of money," ventured Theo.

"It won't last long. I'm so sick and tired of struggling for money all the time. I don't know how—"

"Rae!" Two women and a man stood in front of them.

Rae looked up. Her bleak expression turned to delight. "Cal! And Myrna and Cindy!"

The three sat down on the blanket and they all started talking to Rae at once. "Where have you been all this time? How's it going?"

Finally they noticed Theo. "Do you remember us?" said the woman called Cindy. "We all used to share a house. You were the house baby! You were such a quiet little thing—we barely knew you were there."

Theo shook her head. "I don't remember."

"How old are you now?" asked Myrna. "Six?"

"Nine," muttered Theo.

"You're awfully skinny—you probably don't get enough to eat," said the woman sadly. "I had to give up my little girl, because I couldn't afford to feed her. She's in foster care now. But I'm getting her back one day." Her eyes filled with tears.

"So this is your kid," said Cal. "Hi, there!" He had a handsome face and a wide smile, but his breath reeked of liquor. Theo turned her head. At least Rae didn't drink— she said it made her feel sick.

Theo watched her mother laugh with her friends. The fresh air had turned her cheeks pink and her hair glistened like a golden cloud. Rae would have made a good model or movie star. Perhaps she could have been one—if she hadn't had a baby when she was sixteen.

The friends wandered off. "I'll come and see you at work," the man called.

Rae watched them until they went around the corner. Then she picked up the box of money and counted it. "Twenty-seven dollars! That's because of that first woman. Want to have a hamburger, kid?"

Theo couldn't believe her ears. She hadn't had a meal out since Christmas. They rolled up the tape recorder and the Thermos in the blanket and went into the restaurant on the corner.

Theo gobbled up her cheeseburger. Rae grinned at her. "Good, huh? Take your time—there's plenty more." Now she was in a fantastic mood. The tiny table was loaded with milkshakes and fries and a hamburger each. Rae looked proud that she could afford to give her child all this.

Theo looked around the pink and grey space full of hungry people gorging themselves. A woman smiled at her. Maybe she was thinking, What a happy mother and daughter! Like Caitlin and her mother.

For a moment Theo was only *here*—not wishing or pretending she were somewhere else. Everything was so simple; her hunger was satisfied and her mother was focusing entirely on her.

But then Rae began to go on and on about Cal. "I didn't even know he remembered me! I haven't seen him for four years at least. He was living with Anne-Marie then. Now he's alone. I think he's good-looking, don't you? And he must make decent money, being in construction. Did you hear him say he'd come and see me at work? Do you think he will?"

Rae's face was so hopeful and animated. Theo's full stomach let her feel sorry for her mother. "I'm sure he will," she said.

But she sighed. Now it would begin again—Rae and a new man. Every time her mother found one, she would rave about him for weeks. Then she'd get tired of him and would spend many more weeks complaining about him.

"I think something's going to happen with Cal and me," said her mother. "I can feel it in my bones. I've always liked him, ever since we lived on Rupert Street. He really seemed attracted, don't you think?"

Theo nodded again. Rae was so relaxed, this might be a good moment to bring up the subject of new shoes.

But she'd waited too long. "What am I going to wear if he asks me out?" said Rae. "Let's stop at the Bay basement before we go home—there's enough money left to buy me some earrings."

So much for new shoes. Theo stopped listening. She began staring at a family across the room—two little boys and their parents, who hung on every word they said. The boys began teasing their father about something. They looked like a proper family.

4

Rae began going out with Cal. She got her shift at work changed so she could see him every evening. She would meet Cal after work and come in very late.

Except for Wednesdays and Sundays, Rae's days off, Theo only saw her mother at breakfast. She trudged to school each day and sat in a trance, her head full of the story she'd read the night before. Sometimes Mr. Barker had to shake her shoulder to get her attention. The mean kids gave up calling her "Licehead" and the nice ones gave up being friendly.

Even Angela had given her up, although sometimes she glanced at Theo with a hurt, puzzled expression.

Theo didn't care. It was *safe*, being this invisible. School and home weren't the real world anyhow—they were a dreary grey world that she only *seemed* to exist in.

The real world was the one in books. As soon as she got home from school, Theo fixed herself a quick sandwich or opened some beans and ate them cold from the can.

She would prop open her new library book on the table, then move to the couch, then to bed, reading until she fell asleep.

Now she took home several books at once and got them safely back before Rae noticed. She probably wouldn't have noticed anyway. She, too, was living in another world, a world with only her and Cal in it.

In the morning she'd tell Theo where they'd gone the night before—dancing or to a club. "He's so nice to me!" she said. "He always pays, and he says I look like Julia Roberts. Do you think I do?"

Now Rae was only in bad moods on weekends, when Cal worked on an extra project out of town. On Saturday evenings and Sundays Rae shopped for food and, when she remembered, washed their clothes and hung them out on the balcony to dry. At these times Theo seemed to irritate her more and more.

"Look at these crumbs!" she scolded. "I've told you over and over not to eat in bed. You'll just attract more mice."

The first Sunday in February was particularly bad. The rain gushed out of the sky as if someone had forgotten to turn off a tap. Rae paced around the smoke-filled apartment, complaining endlessly about why Cal couldn't give up his out-of-town job and see more of her.

Theo had finished all her books and was starting one over again—but Rae grabbed it and threw it on the floor so hard its cover came off. "You're always reading! You never listen to me!"

In the evening, after a meagre supper of noodle soup and crackers, Rae seemed ready to burst. Even her usual TV programs couldn't hold her attention.

"There's absolutely nothing to do!"

Theo was staring at the TV screen while her fingers played with the sole of one of her runners. The whole front part had now split. Rae always had new clothes these days—Cal bought them for her.

"Could Cal buy me some new shoes?"

Slap! The blow came so quickly Theo didn't have time to duck. She clutched her burning cheek while tears gathered in her eyes.

"Shoes!" fumed Rae. "Why do you make me feel so guilty all the time? Don't you think I try? Is it my fault your feet grow so fast?"

Theo kept holding her cheek. She wondered if she dared get up and escape to her room.

Then her mother's anger drained out of her and she looked ashamed. "Oh, Kitten … I'm sorry. Give me a hug." Rae reached forward to touch her, but Theo moved to the farthest corner of the couch.

"I just miss Cal so much I can't stand it! I'll tell you what, I'll measure your foot tonight and stop off at Zeller's tomorrow after work, okay?"

Theo didn't answer. It was always like this. The only

times Rae seemed to really care about her were after she had hit her. But those were the times when Theo felt the most removed.

"May I go to my room?" she asked stiffly.

Rae sighed. "Of course. You don't have to treat me like an ogre. It was only a little slap."

She always said that, too.

THE NEXT AFTERNOON Mr. Barker told Theo that the school counsellor wanted to see her. Theo slowly walked down the hall to Ms. Sunter's office.

"Sit down, Theo. How are you today?"

"Fine." Theo slid into a chair in front of Ms. Sunter's desk. How many times had she sat in front of a desk while a nosy adult asked her questions? Sometimes it was a social worker, sometimes a principal or counsellor. Theo examined this one. Ms. Sunter was young and brisk, with pretty black hair and a tailored red pant suit.

She got straight to the point. "Theo, I'm going to ask you some questions and I want you to answer honestly and not be afraid—okay?"

"Okay," said Theo. She braced herself to lie.

"Your teacher says that you are simply not there in class—that you daydream constantly, never do your homework and don't try to make friends. He thought you just needed time to adjust, but you've been here for a month now with no improvement." She smiled. "No one is angry with you. I'm sure there are good reasons why you can't concentrate. Nothing you tell me will get you into trouble, do you understand? I just want to help you." They all said that.

Ms. Sunter rifled through a file of papers. "Now let's see …" She proceeded to recite Theo's history to her, while Theo nodded in the appropriate spots. The names of her previous four schools. The seven places, including two shelters and one hotel, where she and Rae had lived. The times Rae had worked and the times, especially when Theo was a preschooler, when they'd lived on welfare.

Theo stared at the thick file. How did they know so much about her? It made her feel like a criminal with a record.

Ms. Sunter was looking at the pages angrily. "You and your mother have certainly had a hard life. Didn't your father ever help out? Have you ever met him?" Theo shook her head. "Do you know who he is?" asked the counsellor more gently.

Theo squirmed. "He was from Greece. My mother met him when he was staying with his uncle here—she was visiting here too, from Victoria. That's why I have a Greek name," she added. She could hear Rae's words: "As handsome as a Greek god."

Ms. Sunter smiled. "Do you know what your father's name is?"

"Alexios," whispered Theo.

"Alexios what?"

"I don't know. My mother never knew his last name. He was going back to Greece the week after she met him. She didn't have his address and she never heard from him again." Theo flushed. Rae would be furious if she knew she was saying all this.

Ms. Sunter sighed, scribbling in her notes. "I don't know my father either—he left when I was a baby."

"Oh."

Ms. Sunter looked as if she expected her to say more. Theo shifted impatiently and wished the counsellor would get on with the hard part—the questions about Rae.

"Let's talk about your mother now." Theo got ready. "She's working at the Hastings Diner, right?"

"Yes."

"What are her hours?"

"Ten to six."

"Who takes care of you after school?"

Theo thought fast. "A woman in our building called Mrs. Mitic. She's really nice. We watch TV together until my mother comes home."

"Does Mrs. Mitic make your supper?"

"No, my mother does after she gets back from work."

"Do you get enough to eat, Theo? I know your mum must have a hard time stretching her salary."

"My mother's very good at budgeting," said Theo.

"And what sort of things do you have for supper? What did your mother give you last night, for example?"

Theo tried to remember what she'd fixed herself. "Kraft Dinner," she said finally.

Ms. Sunter sighed again. "Yes. A very popular meal."

She asked Theo several questions about the apartment and Theo was careful to say that it was warm and clean.

This was like being on welfare, when every aspect of her and Rae's life was constantly being scrutinized. "They're such snoops!" Rae used to complain. That's why she stayed off welfare whenever she could.

But at least the counsellor wouldn't make a home visit like a social worker would—then she'd find out that Rae was seldom there.

"Theo, I want to ask you something very important now. Is your mother nice to you?"

Theo pretended to look shocked. "Of course!"

"She never hits you?"

"Never," said Theo firmly. She remembered a line from a TV show. "My mother is my best friend."

"That's good to hear. Does she have a boyfriend?"

The question came so fast that Theo didn't have time to lie. "Sort of," she admitted.

"What do you mean?"

"Well, she likes this guy she met in January—but she's only seen him a few times," she added quickly.

"Are you sure, Theo? He doesn't live with you and your mother?"

"No, he doesn't. I told you, she hardly knows him."

"Have you met him?"

"Just once."

"Was he nice to you?"

Theo nodded.

Ms. Sunter studied her and Theo tried not to look down. "Theo, you know that if *anyone*—your mother or her boyfriend or any other adult—was doing anything to you you didn't like, you could tell me. If things ever got really bad at home you could go and live for a while with a family who would take good care of you until your mother was ready to have you back. Would you let me know if you wanted that?"

Theo nodded again, but her face burned.

A foster family—like Myrna had mentioned. Lots of kids lived with foster parents. One girl in Theo's last class said her foster family was mean to her. Another boy was very happy with his.

That was the problem—how would you know what they'd be like if you couldn't choose? And even if the family was nice, you would never really belong to them. Not like being in a real family—not like the families in books.

Now Ms. Sunter was telling her how important it was to work hard in school. "*I* grew up poor, you know. My

47

family lived on welfare for years, but my brother and sister and I all went to university. You can do that too, Theo. I see from your test results that you're very intelligent. Mr. Barker told me you wrote a wonderful poem, and the librarian says you read exceptionally well for a nine-year-old." She smiled. "Perhaps you're a dreamer. That's not a bad thing. But you have to live in *this* world, Theo. Do you think you could start paying attention in class? Could you try a little harder to make some friends?"

Once again, Theo nodded—the way she always did.

"Good. One more thing, Theo. Do you have a shower or a bath in your apartment?"

"A shower," whispered Theo.

Ms. Sunter looked her briskest. "It's a good idea to have a shower and wash your hair every day. Does your mother forget to remind you?"

Theo hung her head. The only times she took a shower were when her hair got so matted she couldn't comb it.

"Your clothes are in bad shape, too," said the counsellor. "I know your mother must have a lot of worries and she can't afford to get you new ones. Did you know we have a free clothing deposit at this school? Let's go and pick out some things for you."

She took Theo's hand and they went along the hall to a locked room. Ms. Sunter opened the door and found a lot of clothes for Theo—a patterned red sweater, two pairs of jeans, T-shirts, a sweatshirt and a quilted green jacket with only a few stains on it. Best of all was a pair of pink high-top runners that were just a bit too big for her.

Theo wriggled her toes in the roomy shoes. She exchanged her skimpy sweater for the warm red one. Ms. Sunter put the rest of the clothes in a bag. "You can leave it in my office until after school," she said.

"Thank you," whispered Theo.

Ms. Sunter shook her hand. "It's been a pleasure to meet you, Theo. Let's have another talk next month. But you can knock at my door any time, all right?"

Ms. Sunter was *nice*, decided Theo, as she walked back to the classroom, looking down at her new pink shoes all the way. Ms. Sunter understood what it was like to be poor.

But she and the counsellor had forgotten that the other kids would immediately notice Theo's change of clothing. Some looked at her with pity and some with disdain as she slid into her seat.

RAE WAS ANGRY when she saw the clothes. "Do they think I can't take care of you? I bought you some shoes, didn't I?" Rae had come home for dinner and presented Theo with a brand new pair of navy runners. She wanted Theo to take back the pink ones.

"Oh, please—can't I keep them both?"

"Well … all right," grumbled Rae, getting dressed to go out again. "But don't accept any more of their charity or they'll start checking up on us."

Theo took both pairs of shoes to bed with her. She couldn't decide which ones she liked the best. The pink ones were more in style but the white rubber on the navy ones was so smooth and clean. She couldn't remember ever having two pairs of shoes. She decided she would wear the navy ones tomorrow and the pink ones the next day.

After she turned out her light, Theo thought about her talk with Ms. Sunter. She was relieved the counsellor hadn't found out how she really lived—but if only she *could* help her. If only she could somehow find Theo a real family, not to stay with temporarily, but to live with always.

She hugged Sabrina and went over the familiar details.

Four children, two boys and two girls … Theo would share a room with the two girls and after they went to bed they would whisper and giggle and tell each other secrets …

"KITTEN, I have something to tell you. Cal and I are going away for the weekend," Rae said the next morning.

"Going away? Where?"

"To Harrison Hot Springs. Cal has the weekend off and he has a friend who has a cabin there we can use."

"What about me?" said Theo. "What will I do?"

Rae looked evasive. "You can stay here, can't you? It's only for two nights. Donna's working Saturday for me. We're leaving Friday after work and we'll be back on

Sunday night. Mrs. Mitic will keep an eye on you, and I'll get you lots of treats to eat."

Theo shivered. "Please, Rae … I don't want to stay here alone. Can't I come with you?"

Rae drained her coffee, her eyes down. "The trouble is, Cal doesn't really feel comfortable around kids. And we need a little time to be by ourselves."

She looked up. "I know you want to come, Kitten, but this is really important to me." Her eyes pleaded so strongly that Theo stopped objecting.

She tried to persuade herself how great it would be to wallow in books all weekend. She could open all the windows and clear the apartment of Rae's smoke. But all she felt was panic.

WHEN RAE CAME HOME on Sunday, Theo was lying in a stupor in front of the TV, surrounded by dirty plates, empty potato chip bags and candy wrappers. Her head pounded and her stomach hurt from eating so much of the junk food Rae had left for her.

Mrs. Mitic had poked her head in yesterday afternoon. "Are you all right, girl?" When Theo had nodded, she'd asked her to go to the store and get her some coffee. At least that had been something to do; already her head was too heavy to read any more.

She'd managed to hang around Mrs. Mitic's apartment for the rest of the day, watching a movie with her. But at supper-time the old woman had shooed her down the hall. "All right, that's enough of you. I want to phone my sister. You know where I am if you need anything."

She'd been so brusque that Theo hadn't gone back, even though the second night was just as awful as the first. She couldn't escape into sleep from her night terrors, not when she knew Rae wasn't arriving home later. Theo quivered in bed, sure that every sound was something coming to get her. She didn't close her eyes until the first sign of light; then she had a terrible nightmare about falling down a dark hole, falling forever without landing.

Today she had hardly left the couch, letting the TV sound fill up the empty space inside her. She couldn't read and she couldn't pretend; she was a grey blob of nothing.

Now Theo looked up at her mother blearily. At least she wasn't alone any more.

Rae looked sort of—*sparkly*. Her cheeks glowed and her hair was dotted with raindrops. She moved away some of the encrusted plates, sat down beside Theo and gave her a hug. Theo stiffened.

"I have wonderful news, Kitten. Cal has asked me to move in with him!"

Theo felt as if all the air had been sucked out of her. "What?"

"He's asked me to live with him—isn't that cool? I've

finally found the right man! He's really committed, Theo, I can tell."

"But—" Theo couldn't get her tongue around the question. Finally it blurted out. "But what about me? Will I live there, too?"

Rae had never looked so guilty. "We haven't made up our minds about that yet." She shook her wet hair as if she were shaking away the decision. "But don't worry, Kitten. I have a plan—I just need to figure out the details. It will all work out, I promise. Whatever happens, I'll make sure you're taken good care of."

5

"*Please*, Rae—I don't want to go!" begged Theo for the hundredth time.

Rae was shoving Theo's clothes into a duffel bag. She looked up, holding a blue sock. "Theo, we've been over this again and again. I've told you, it's only for a little while. Just until Cal and I get settled. Then I'll persuade him to let you live with us. But he isn't ready for you yet—he needs to get used to me first. Don't you see, Kitten? Besides, Sharon really wants you. She was overjoyed when I suggested it."

"I don't *know* Sharon," moaned Theo.

"Of course you know her. She's your aunt! She was always making a fuss over you when you lived with her and Ma. Is there a mate for this sock?"

Theo ran out of the room and buried her face in the couch. It was no use. She'd argued angrily with Rae all week, ever since she'd phoned Sharon in Victoria.

Surprisingly, Rae didn't get angry back. She repeated

her arguments with a wooden patience, as if she were learning lines for a play. Theo wanted to scream every time she said, "It's only for a little while."

Exactly how long was a "little while"? Every time she asked, Rae would repeat, "I can't say exactly. We just have to wait and see."

The only thing that was certain was that tomorrow—tomorrow!—she and Rae were taking the ferry to Victoria. Rae was leaving her there. Leaving her to live with her older sister Sharon, whom Theo couldn't remember at all.

Wasn't that what she yearned for? To live somewhere else? But not this! She wanted a *family*, a proper family with a mother and a father and four children—not a single aunt. And what would Sharon be like? What if she was mean? And she'd have to start a new school again …

Rae wouldn't let her tell anyone that she was going to Victoria at the end of the week. "They might start interfering," she said. "Later I'll write the school a note and say you've left temporarily."

But Theo knew that, once again, she was being yanked out of a school for good. Even if she did come back, Rae and Cal would be living in another part of the city.

She didn't like this school, not any more than she had liked any of them. But she had become used to it. She always stood alone in the same place at recess and ate by herself in the same chair at lunch. And this school had the best library—she'd miss that most of all.

Theo wondered what would happen if she went to Ms. Sunter and told her Rae's plan. Maybe she could do something. But maybe Ms. Sunter would arrange to take Theo away from Rae and put her in a foster home. That would be just as scary as going to live with Sharon.

There was no solution. All week Theo was too miserable to daydream. She sat at her desk and looked around the classroom with a pounding head. She'd miss all this—the gerbils scuffling at the back of the room, the smell of chalk and boys' sweaty socks, the frieze of everyone's handprints above the blackboard. She would even miss Mr. Barker's bounciness and Angela's shy smiles. At least school was *something*—ahead of her was nothing.

Theo curled herself into a tight ball on the couch and refused to speak to Rae for the rest of their last evening together. That night in bed she clutched Sabrina and sobbed into her pillow so Rae wouldn't hear.

CAL HAD TAKEN the day off to drive them to the ferry on Sunday. He was supposed to come at 11:30, but he still wasn't there at one o'clock.

There was nothing to do but wait. Rae had washed all of Theo's clothes and made Theo have a shower. She combed out her wet hair, complaining at the tangles. All Theo's things were packed in the bulging duffel bag sitting at the door. Rae paced and smoked, while Theo sat motionless, wishing with all her might that Cal wouldn't come at all.

Just as Rae was about to use Mrs. Mitic's phone and call him, Cal appeared at the door.

"Sorry," he muttered. "Something came up." He kissed Rae and glanced at Theo. "How're you doing, kid?"

Theo turned away from his beery breath. She hated everything about him. She hated the way he pushed back his perfect hair in the mirror before they left and the way his boots pounded on the stairs as he carried down Theo's bag.

You are a *beetle*, she decided, watching his long legs in their tight black jeans scuttle down ahead of her. A black beetle I could squash with my shoe.

Most of all she hated the way Rae acted around him. She didn't even complain that he was over two hours late. She sat beside him on the front seat and kept her hand on the back of his neck all the way to the ferry, tickling and caressing it. Sometimes Cal leaned over and kissed her hair, and sometimes they sang together to the words of the loud music on the radio.

They were disgusting. Theo tried to pretend they weren't there. She stared out the window as they made their way out of Vancouver and through a long scary tunnel that roared with car engines. The traffic increased until all the cars seemed to be having a race to the ferry. They sped past flat fields dotted with barns, horses and cows. Suddenly the sea appeared, dim mountains in the distance, and they followed the line of cars across a long spit that led over the water like a bridge to the ferry terminal.

Cal dropped them off at the foot-passenger entrance. He gave Rae a long lingering kiss. Then he held out his hand to Theo. "Goodbye, kid. Have fun."

Theo yanked her hand out of his grasp and wiped it on her jeans. Cal shrugged and told Rae that he'd see her tomorrow.

THEY WERE JUST IN TIME for the three-o'clock ferry. Theo and Rae had to run along a glass-covered ramp, holding the handles of the duffel bag between them. They stepped onto the huge boat, found two seats in the front of a lounge, and collapsed, catching their breaths.

Theo looked around with wide eyes. She must have been on a ferry before, when Rae had come to get her from Victoria when she was three—but she couldn't remember it.

There were only three seats in their row. A teenager beside Rae was tapping his foot to a tune from the earphones he had on. Across the aisle people were opening up newspapers and books and cans of pop. The large room was surrounded by windows. Theo was beside one; she could see people walking around on the deck outside.

The enormous boat was vibrating. Then a two-toned beep on a loudspeaker made Theo jump, as a strident female voice began announcing the sailing time to Victoria and the services on board. There was a whistle, a pause, deeper vibrating, and then the ship began to move. It backed out of its berth while the announcer talked about lifeboats, then gradually turned around.

Rae was in a foul mood. "I don't see why the whole ferry is non-smoking now," she grumbled. "It didn't use to be." She tapped the arm of her chair. "I'd like to get back early tomorrow," she said. "I hope Sharon doesn't expect me to stay just because I got the day off."

Sharon … Theo was trying hard not to think of her, but now that she'd lost the fight she couldn't help asking, "What's she like?"

"My sister? She's okay, I suppose. She was always a goody-goody. *She* never got into trouble. The nuns adored her."

"Nuns?"

"The nuns at the school we went to."

"Are you Catholic?" asked Theo with surprise.

Rae chuckled. "Well, I *was*, so I guess I still am. Once a Catholic, always a Catholic, my father used to say. You won't catch me inside a church, though. But I bet Sharon still goes. She'll probably take you, too."

Theo pondered this. She'd never been inside a church before. "Why haven't I ever met Sharon?" she asked.

"Theo, you have! I keep telling you! You lived with her and Ma until you were three!"

Theo flushed. Rae was speaking so loud that people were staring at them.

A woman standing by the window in front of them stared especially hard. She was tall and angular, with messy hair and a baggy tweed coat. She kept on staring even after she noticed Theo looking back at her.

Theo turned her head away from the nosy woman. "I know I lived with Sharon," she said quickly, to make Rae lower her voice. "I meant, why haven't I seen her since then?"

Rae looked guilty. "Oh, I don't know. I guess because I never told her where we lived. I thought she'd try to interfere."

"She probably wanted to see me, though," said Theo boldly.

"I'm sure she did. She had a fit when I took you away. Well, now she will see you. If you feel that strongly about Sharon, why don't you want to live with her?"

Theo's eyes stung with tears. She leaned down to unzip the duffel bag. She'd managed to bring home a library book without signing it out. It was stealing, she supposed, but she didn't care.

Rae watched her for a few seconds. "I'm sorry, Kitten," she sighed. "That was unfair. I know you don't want to go. Listen, I can't help this. It won't be forever—"

Now Theo had to raise her voice. "I don't want to talk about it!" The woman at the window was still watching and listening. Theo lowered her face and hid behind her book.

"Theo, please try to understand!" Her mother sounded close to tears, but Theo kept her head down. "I just can't cope! I've tried my best, but I'm so tired of trying alone! I'm only twenty-five—why shouldn't I have a chance to be happy? Someone I really love loves me back. And he has enough money to take care of both of us. I can't risk losing him! If I play my cards right, I won't. Once he gets used to me, I *promise* I'll come for you. But for now you have to live with Sharon. It won't be that bad. Sharon's a lot nicer than I am—she always has been. I bet you'll like her. Theo? Kitten? Are you listening to me?"

The words on the page were blurry, but Theo kept her head lowered and her eyes fixed on the book.

Rae waited a few seconds. "Theo, *look* at me!" Now her voice was angry. Theo could feel the heat of her mother's temper like a flaring flame beside her. She quaked inside, but surely Rae wouldn't slap her in public. She kept her head still.

"All right, then." Rae's voice was a furious mutter. "You can stay with Sharon, for all I care. You never listen to what I say. Well, now you won't have to listen to me at all!"

She stood up. "I'm going out to the deck to have a smoke. Don't you dare move from that seat." She pushed past the teenager into the aisle. Theo lifted her eyes only and watched her leave the lounge.

When she was sure Rae was gone, she closed the book and leaned back against the seat, trembling and trying not to cry. She looked out the side window and saw Rae's back, leaning over the railing of the deck with a cigarette between her fingers. She took short, angry puffs of it, threw it overboard, and stomped out of sight along the deck.

Theo kept staring out the window. If only her mother would never come back! If only Theo were sitting here in the midst of her brothers and sisters. Two boys and two girls …

She closed her eyes. *What would their names be? Maybe John for the oldest, like the John in the Ransome books. The other boy could be Timothy, and the girls would be called Rosalind and Rosemary … or maybe Suzanne and Samara … The girls would look like their mother and the boys like their father …*

Never had Theo yearned for a real family so much. As long as she kept her eyes closed she could *see* them—four children and two parents talking and laughing around her. With Theo securely in the middle.

But of course when she opened her eyes Theo was still alone. The lounge full of people was a bright blur through her tears. The boy beside her was opening a bag of chips.

And that nosy woman was still staring at her! Her

glittering eyes pierced right through Theo. They seemed full of compassion and curiosity—and excitement, as if she knew Theo from somewhere.

Why was she still standing there? She didn't seem to mind that Theo noticed her rudeness. Theo felt flushed, as if the woman had found out something about her. She wiped her eyes and pretended to read. When she looked up again the woman had gone.

PART 2

The Family

6

Theo waited in a numb trance for Rae to come back. Being on the ferry was a nothing time, before the next awful thing that would happen. She felt as empty and lost as a husk that someone had thrown away. It was no use wishing that her life was different. It was no use wishing for a family. It didn't matter what happened to her. *She* didn't matter.

She noticed listlessly that the lounge was more crowded. Toddlers reeled up and down the aisles, followed by protective parents. All around her kids leaned over the backs of chairs, asked for food or demanded money for the arcade. A little girl walked by chanting, "Follow the pink, follow the pink," as she balanced on the strip of pink in the green carpeting. She paused by Theo's chair and swung on one of the skinny poles that dotted the room.

A group of small boys had assembled on the rug between the windows and the front row where Theo sat, kneeling over tiny cars. Other little kids joined them as if magnetized, their older brothers and sisters watching from the sides. It was as if all the kids on the ferry belonged to a tribe—all except Theo.

"John, wait up!"

John? Something quickened in Theo's empty insides as she heard the familiar name.

She turned around swiftly.

Four children were coming up the aisle—two boys and two girls. The oldest boy held a much younger boy by the hand. Behind them was another girl. A smaller girl was running to catch up with them. "John!" she called again to the older boy. "Mummy says don't go outside without jackets."

"We're not going out yet," said John. "Ben wants to see what these kids are doing."

Theo felt a twinge of disappointment that the youngest boy wasn't called Timothy. But that didn't matter. She trembled as the four gathered right in front of her.

Ben and the younger girl dropped to the floor and joined the gang of little kids there. John and the other girl stood by the window, smiling at their brother and sister.

John had light brown hair that hung like a curtain on each side of his face. His ears and hands and feet looked too big for his skinny body.

His sister was the same height—were they twins? Her hair was shorter and darker than John's, cut in a shining cap. She had a wide mouth that glittered with braces.

Theo shifted her gaze to the other two. Ben was engrossed in building something with another child. His hair was the same colour as John's, but it curled around his chubby face, which was sprinkled with freckles. His sister was organizing a clapping game with three other children. She was the prettiest, with a long blonde pony-tail and huge fringed eyes. She looked delicate beside her sturdy little brother.

"Lisbeth, stop being so bossy," said the older girl.

"But they aren't playing it right!"

"Let them play it the way they want to."

Ben looked up. "Anna, I need to blow my nose."

Theo hugged her knees as Anna handed Ben a tissue. Now she knew all their names—John, Anna, Lisbeth and Ben.

A proper family. A family of four! She forgot her misery as she drank in every detail, trembling with wonder.

They seemed just the right ages, with a gap between Anna and Lisbeth for Theo to fit into. Anna looked kind, and John looked sort of … *noble*. Lisbeth was obviously mischievous and little Ben was cuddly, like a teddy bear. They were perfect.

Watching them was like reading about them in a book—except it wasn't a book. The family was real— standing right in front of her!

Theo had a daring idea. Maybe she could get to know them. Maybe she could actually speak to them.

Why not? All the other kids were chatting easily. This wasn't school. No one knew anything about each other, so the usual barriers were gone.

Theo glanced out the window. Rae was nowhere in sight. She slid out of her seat and edged closer and closer to Anna. John was helping Ben with something on the floor.

Say something. But it was so hard. Theo couldn't make her tongue work and her legs kept shaking.

Then Anna noticed her and smiled—a large, friendly smile. "Hi."

"Hi," gulped Theo.

"What's your name?"

"Theo Caffrey," whispered Theo.

"I'm Anna—Anna Kaldor. Do you live in Victoria?"

Theo shook her head.

"Vancouver?"

Theo just stood there. How could she explain that, at the moment, she didn't live anywhere at all?

Anna didn't persist. "We live in Victoria, but we've been visiting our grandparents in West Vancouver for the weekend. It was my grannie's seventieth birthday. We got to miss a day of school and come on Friday." She had a calm, warm voice.

Lisbeth jumped up and joined them. "Who's that, Anna?"

"Don't point, Lisbeth. This is Theo. This is Lisbeth, my rude little sister. And those two are my brothers."

"Now *you're* pointing." Lisbeth took a pack of cards out of her pocket. "Do you want to play Fish with us?" To Theo's astonishment Lisbeth pulled her by the hand.

"Come on, John and Ben," she ordered. "We're playing Fish."

"We always do what Lisbeth says," grinned Anna. All four of them sat down in a circle. Theo was part of it.

She was introduced to John and Ben. John nodded at her; he seemed shy. Ben pulled up a black patch on a piece of elastic around his neck and fixed it over one eye. He put his hand on a plastic dagger stuck in his belt and tugged at Theo's sweater.

"Are you a pirate?" guessed Theo. He nodded proudly.

Theo held her cards in a fan and tried to stop her fingers from trembling as they all took turns asking for fives or jacks or sevens. Ben sprawled in Anna's lap, gripping her cards. She kept burying her face in his curls. He ignored her, like a little prince used to homage.

"Lisbeth's looking at our cards," he complained.

"I can't help it! You aren't holding them up!"

"They're too big," said Ben. The cards were almost falling out of his small hands.

"Let him put his cards on the floor. No one will look at them, Ben," said John.

"I will," said Lisbeth. "How can I help it, if they're just lying there?"

"Then you're a cheat!" said Ben.

"I am not!"

"Shhh! If you're going to argue, let's stop. Fish is boring, anyway," said Anna. They began making houses out of the cards instead. John was the best at balancing four cards against each other, then laying another on top for a roof.

Now Lisbeth was asking Theo where she lived. She had to say *something*. "I—uh—my mother and I live in Vancouver. We're going to Victoria to visit my aunt." That seemed to satisfy them.

"Do you like iguanas?" asked Ben.

"I guess so," said Theo with surprise. She wasn't quite sure what an iguana was. Some kind of lizard?

"I have a *huge* iguana. He's this long." He held out his arms as far as they would go. "His name's Mortimer."

Lisbeth put her mouth close to Theo's ear. "He doesn't really have an iguana," she whispered. "He just pretends he does, because our parents say he's not old enough for one."

Ben frowned at her. "Mortimer's *fierce*. He's as fierce as a—as a tyrannosaurus rex! Bingo's afraid of him. That's our dog. He's in the car because dogs aren't allowed upstairs on the ferry."

"*I* have a guinea pig," said Lisbeth. "Her name's Snow White and she's going to have babies."

"I don't think she is, Lisbeth," said John. He grinned at Anna. "You need two guinea pigs for babies. I think she's just fat."

"She's having babies," insisted Lisbeth. "About six or seven, I think. All their names are going to be after the seven dwarves. Grumpy and Sleepy and Dopey and—"

Anna interrupted her. "We have a cat, too. He's called Beardsley."

"I have sixteen fish," said John. He looked worried. "I hope the Mitchells remembered to come in and feed them."

Theo's ears and eyes couldn't stretch large enough to take all of this in. She sat quietly in the middle of the group, feeling amazingly relaxed.

Lisbeth's violet-blue eyes were looking at her curiously. "How old are you?"

"Nine," said Theo.

"I'm seven," said Lisbeth. "Ben is only four. Anna's ten and John's twelve. In the fall he'll be a teenager! He'll start staying out late and getting into trouble."

John frowned. "You're the one who's trouble."

Theo continued to let their banter wash over her like a warm wave. This was it! This was the family she'd dreamed about. She ached to belong to them—to be their sister.

But how could she? Magic was only in stories. She couldn't wish to belong to them and have it come true. Her emptiness twitched at her, as if it were reminding her that it was still there—that she didn't belong anywhere.

There wasn't time to worry about it. At the moment, at least, this family seemed to accept Theo as part of them. They swept her along in their energy.

"We're almost at Active Pass—let's go outside," said John.

"Come on!" said Ben. He grabbed Theo's hand—the second time one of them had touched her. His palm was pudgy and hot.

"Can you?" asked Anna. "Should you ask your mother?"

Rae. Theo had completely forgotten her. "She's already outside, having a cigarette," she told them. "But she said— she said I could go and look for her when I wanted," she finished quickly.

"Then let's go!" said Lisbeth.

"Bring your jacket, Theo. We have to get ours," said Anna.

Theo snatched up her jacket and followed them down the aisle, to a man and woman sitting near the back. They looked up from their books and smiled.

"This is our brand new friend," said Lisbeth.

"Her name's Theo," said Ben.

"How do you do, Theo?" The woman leaned forward and shook her hand as if she were a grown-up. "I'm Laura Rice and this is my husband, Dan Kaldor." They looked as perfect as their children. Laura was small, with tidy brown hair. Dan was round and rumpled-looking, with a beard and glasses.

"We're going out," said Anna, pulling on a purple fleece jacket.

"Do your parents know where you are, Theo?" Laura asked.

"Her mother's already on the deck—we're going to look for her," said John.

"Okay. Be sure to stay together," said Dan.

The five of them raced out to the deck.

THEY STOOD IN A ROW by the railing, the icy wind whipping back their hair. Beyond them was a tossing kaleidoscope of water and land and sky. The huge boat was making its way towards a channel between two rocky islands studded with firs and small houses. The sea was almost the same grey-blue as the sky; fishing boats bobbed on its swelling surface.

Another long white ferry was approaching on the opposite side of the pass. The children covered their ears as the boat's whistle blared.

Lisbeth and Ben waved frantically to the other ferry

as it glided by. Then Lisbeth whirled around. "Let's *fly*!" she shouted.

She tore along the wide deck, the others following. Towards the bow the wind was so strong they had to push against it, while their legs walked in slow motion.

"*Fly!*" screamed Lisbeth. She opened up her jacket and held it out. "Come on, Theo, you do it, too!"

Theo unzipped her jacket and gasped as the wind slapped her chest like a huge cold hand. Her eyes streamed and her hair felt ripped out by its roots. But she copied the others and held the sides of her jacket open like wings. The wind actually lifted her a little off the ground—then she fell backwards onto the deck.

"Are you okay?" Anna helped her up.

Theo nodded. She tried again, and this time she kept her balance.

"*Flyyy …*" They jumped and twisted and danced in the wind's power. Lisbeth was lifted the highest, as if she were a feather. At first John had hung back but soon he was shouting as loudly as the others.

"Let's go and scare Mummy and Daddy!" said Ben. Their feet thundered along the deck as they dashed back and pounded on the windows beside the place where their parents were sitting. The whole row of adults jerked with surprise. Dan wagged his finger and Laura waved them away.

They battled their way to the side of the ferry, where it

was less windy. There they stopped to zip up their jackets and catch their breaths. They held onto the cold bars of the railing and peered at the sheet of water far below. Beyond them rose the cliffs at the end of one of the islands.

"I wonder why we haven't seen your mother yet, Theo," said Anna.

Theo had been relieved they hadn't run into Rae. "Maybe she's on another deck," she said hopefully.

"Shouldn't we go and look for her?" asked John.

Theo put up her hood to warm her freezing ears—and to give her time to think. "We can wait a while," she said. "It's okay. She won't be worried." She had almost added, "She doesn't care." She watched some gulls hovering in the sky as if they were pasted there.

"How long are you staying in Victoria?" asked Anna.

"I don't know."

"Maybe you'll have time to come and visit us."

"We have our own mountain!" said Ben.

"It's just a rocky hill behind our house, but Ben calls it a mountain," explained John.

"And in front we have a *graveyard*," said Lisbeth. "It's spooky!"

"Don't scare her," said Anna. "Our house is across the street from a cemetery, Theo. It's not spooky at all. It's like a park and we play there every day."

"Could you come and play with us when you're in Victoria?" asked Ben.

"Could you? Please?" begged Lisbeth.

"When we go back in we'll give you our address," said Anna. "Maybe your mum could bring you over."

Theo gazed at the Kaldors' friendly faces. "I'll try," she said softly. But she wondered if Sharon would let her go.

"Hurray!" Lisbeth threw her arms around Theo and hugged her hard. An icy part of Theo melted and she tentatively hugged Lisbeth back.

"Look at the moon!" cried Ben. "The moon in the daytime!" He pointed to a sliver of pale moon.

"Why does it look like it's moving?" said Lisbeth.

"Because *we're* moving," said John. "It's a new moon."

"How do you know?" demanded Lisbeth.

"Because it's shaped like a backwards C. We learned that last year."

"Grannie says you can wish on a new moon," said Anna.

"*I'm* going to wish," said Ben. He squeezed his eyes shut.

"I bet you're wishing for a real iguana," said Lisbeth. "Let's all wish."

The five of them looked up at the moon while the ferry churned its way to Victoria.

I wish I could belong to this family, thought Theo. But the wish made her want to cry—it would never come true.

Then she looked towards the bow. Rae was striding

around the corner, struggling with the wind. She caught sight of Theo and headed towards her.

Theo almost screamed with despair. She couldn't go with Rae to Victoria and be left with an unknown aunt! An aunt who was probably mean, who'd probably never let her visit the Kaldors. She couldn't lose this family just as she had found them!

Her mother was coming closer and closer. Theo had never seen her look so angry.

She looked back at the moon and wished out loud. "*Please*! I wish I belonged to this family right *now*!"

7

Something was dripping. A steady soft splash close to her. Theo opened her eyes.

She was cocooned in rose-coloured flannelette—sheets, pillowcase and fluffy quilt. She stretched out her legs and wriggled her toes. It was like being in a warm nest.

Theo turned over on her back. Above the bed was a skylight shaded with a striped blue and white blind. Rain was dripping onto it; that's what had woken her.

No … she couldn't be awake. She must be dreaming she was awake.

She turned her eyes to the large room. Opposite her was a set of bunk beds, a bunched-up quilt strewn on each one. One pillow was on the floor, the other, patterned with alphabet letters, hanging precariously over the edge of the mattress. Each bed was crowded with stuffed animals.

On the wall opposite her was a large poster of a hockey player and a smaller one of a running horse.

The floor was thick with stuff. Swimming goggles, a purple plastic purse, a red and yellow backpack, various shoes, a drinking straw twisted into a treble clef, an empty plastic bag, a small book closed with a padlock, a broken Slinky, many clothes and a tape recorder. A large cardboard box overflowed with Barbie doll paraphernalia. Balled-up tissues and gum wrappers surrounded an empty wastepaper basket.

The walls were lined with shelves decorated with stickers. The higher ones were crammed with books and magazines, model horses and two china piggy banks. On the lower shelves were more books, notepads, straw baskets overflowing with jewellery and shells, a snow dome, a pink dinosaur, a photograph of a lot of girls dressed in soccer uniforms, a baseball glove and dozens of hair elastics. Two dressers were against the far wall, their tops strewn with more stuff and most of their drawers gaping open.

From the ceiling were suspended a rooster puppet on strings and two mobiles, one of felt flowers and one of whales. A poster labelled "My Grow Chart" went up one wall and all around the top of it ran a peeling frieze of Beatrix Potter characters.

Theo kept gazing at the colourful chaos. Then she

sat up gingerly; she didn't want to wake herself up. She glanced at the table beside the bed and gasped.

"THEO!" Her name shouted at her from the top of a piece of paper.

She picked it up and read with trembling fingers.

Good morning! We hope you're feeling better.
Mum and Dad said we had to go to school, so
we won't see you until lunch. I've put a housecoat
and slippers for you on the chair. Mum is
working in the room at the back of the kitchen.
She says to come down when you're ready for
breakfast. Can't wait to see you again!

Love, Anna.

Theo tried to steady her breath. Had it happened? The last thing she could remember was standing on the windy deck of the ferry, while Rae strode towards her. Then Theo had made a desperate wish on the new moon. Wishing she could be in this family …

Had her wish come true? But how was that possible? She *must* be dreaming! She pinched the skin on the back of her hand—it hurt.

"It *has* happened!" she whispered. She felt ripped open with joy.

She stood on the bed and tugged at the blind covering

the skylight. It shot up with a rattle, exposing tree branches dripping with water.

Now the colourful room was even brighter. A blue housecoat and furry red slippers lay on a chair beside the bed. Theo stepped onto the bare wood floor. She looked down—she was wearing red pyjamas she'd never seen before. They were too big and the sleeves and legs dangled below her hands and feet. She rolled them up and put on the housecoat and slippers.

The fat slippers made her feet look like red cushions. She padded around the messy room. The bottom bunk must be Lisbeth's—a small pink nightgown was scrunched on it. A beautiful, new-looking doll was leaning against the headboard. It had red hair and a tartan dress edged with lace. Theo picked it up, touched each of the doll's shiny black shoes, and inhaled its clean rubbery smell. Then she put it back in the same place, smoothing its long hair.

A movement at the end of the bed make her squeal. What she thought was a stuffed animal stretched out its legs and raised its head.

A cat! A black and white cat with long legs. It came over and sniffed at Theo, purring. She patted it gently, trying to remember its name—Moustache?

Beardsley, that was it. "Hello, Beardsley," whispered Theo. The cat arched its back, pressing its head against her hand. She rubbed it in the hollow places behind its ears, the way she used to with Calico Cat.

Then she had to pee. She went out of the bedroom into a square hall and found the bathroom off it. It was as untidy as the girls' room, with damp towels in a heap on the floor and small pieces of bright plastic—Lego, a frog, boats—strewn in the bathtub and sink.

After Theo came out, she stood gloating for a few seconds in the middle of the hall. If she peed in a dream she'd wake up in a wet bed. But she was still here!

She glanced into the other open doors. One room was a grown-up's containing a wide, neatly made bed. The other room smelled like dirty socks. It was littered with little boys' clothes and toys and contained only one narrow bed. Ben must sleep here; she wondered where John's room was.

The house was very quiet. Some faint car noises came from outside and a gurgling sound came from below. Theo hesitated at the top of the stairs, staring at the blurry view beyond the window: a holly hedge, layers of treetops and a leaden sky. Her stomach roared with hunger, but she felt too shy to talk to the children's mother alone. What was her name? Laura …

Then Theo's ecstasy faded as quickly as it had come. She was sure Laura would tell Theo she didn't really belong here. It was silly to think that her wish had come true. There was probably a reason she was in this house. Rae might have got sick on the ferry and Theo had come here to stay for a few days. Or maybe Rae—or

Sharon—gave her permission to visit. But why couldn't she remember?

Finally she worked up enough nerve to go down the stairs. They led into another hall. On one side was a living-room, on the other a den lined with books. Theo kept following the hall to a large kitchen with a smaller room at the far end of it. Through the open door she could see a woman sitting at a table, her back to Theo.

A big black dog leapt up from the woman's feet and galumphed over to Theo. It jumped up and slathered her face with its tongue, its thrashing tail hitting the wall. Theo backed away; she had always avoided dogs.

"Down, Bingo! Come here!" Laura hurried over and took the dog by its collar. "You're awake, Theo! I hope you don't mind dogs. He's very gentle—he's just kissing you. *Bed*, Bingo!" The dog went over to a large round cushion in the corner of the kitchen; but he kept his eyes hopefully on Theo.

Theo wiped her face. A kiss? It was more like a wash.

"Did you have a good sleep?" asked Laura. "Do you feel better?"

Theo nodded with confusion. Had she been sick?

"You must be starving—it's almost eleven! Come and sit down and I'll get you some breakfast. Would you like cereal? Toast?"

Theo sat at a scratched wooden table and gulped down a bowl of puffed rice. Then she ate two pieces of toast and peanut butter and an orange cut into sections. She sipped at a mug of cocoa, her stomach finally satisfied.

Laura didn't seem to mind that Theo didn't speak. Her movements were precise and orderly as she buttered toast and poured cocoa into the mug. Her smooth dark hair met in points below her narrow chin; her long fingers were stained yellow and red.

"Feel better?" She sat down beside Theo with a mug of coffee. "We had a hard time getting the others off to school! Lisbeth wanted you to go with them, but you're supposed to take it easy. Did you know you fainted? Luckily there was a doctor on the ferry. You weren't out for very long, but as soon as you came to, you went right to sleep. You slept all the way back to the city in the car. We had to carry you up to bed. Do you remember fainting?"

Theo shook her head. Why had she been brought to this house? Where was Rae? She waited for Laura to tell her, but Laura just sat there calmly, smiling at Theo.

Theo tried to think of something to say besides asking where her mother was. "Where's Ben?" she asked finally. Surely he was too young to go to school.

"Ben goes to preschool every morning. My neighbour brings him home at twelve. And Dan's at work. He teaches English at the University of Victoria. I work at home—I'm a graphic artist. Right now I'm doing a line of greeting cards. I'll show them to you later."

So that was why her fingers were stained.

Laura leaned forward, her eyes full of affection. "Dan and I have been discussing what you should call us, Theo. Of course we aren't your real parents, but since you're part of this family now, do you want to call us Mum and Dad like the others do? Or would you prefer Laura and Dan … It's entirely up to you, and you don't have to decide right away."

Theo almost fell off her chair. "Part of this family now." Then it *had* happened! But how? How could she possibly just wish on the new moon and have her wish come true? Even in a book that would seem unbelievable.

But Theo didn't want to think about how or why. She was *here*, in this safe, cozy house. Somehow her wish had come true—a pleasant woman was sitting beside her and asking Theo if she wanted to call her "Mum."

Maybe it would all turn out to be a dream, or to have some other explanation. Maybe this would end as suddenly as it began. In that case she was going to soak up as much of this wonderful adventure as she could, before it was snatched away.

"If you don't mind … I'd like to call you Mum and Dad," Theo whispered.

"Are you sure? You don't want to think about it?"

"I'm sure."

There were tears in Laura's eyes. "I would be honoured if you would, Theo." She kissed her cheek gently. "Now you really are part of us."

Theo felt herself melt, just as she had on the ferry when Lisbeth had hugged her. This was magic. Her legs were wobbly and she could hardly stand up when Laura suggested they go upstairs and find some clothes. "The others will be home for lunch soon."

Laura took Theo's hand and led her out of the kitchen. Bingo followed them with a ball in his mouth. When they reached the upstairs hall, he dropped it in front of Theo. He looked so eager that she picked it up, gooey with saliva, and threw it down the stairs. He rushed after it and was back instantly. Theo reached out and timidly stroked his head. His black fur was as soft as velvet and his adoring brown eyes begged her to throw the ball again.

"Just ignore him," said Laura. "He'll never leave you alone if you don't." She sighed as they entered the girls' room. "I'm the only neat person in this sloppy family. All Dan keeps in order are his books, and the rest of them are hopeless." She began picking up the clothes on the floor. "I hope you don't mind sharing a room with Anna and Lisbeth, Theo. At least they had this extra bed. Dan just converted a storage cupboard downstairs for John. It's minute, but he loves being on his own—he used to share with Ben. I wish we had more space, but we love this old house so much we'd never leave it. Now let's see ... you're in between Anna and Lisbeth for sizes. There's not much that's going to fit."

Laura poked around in the drawers and the closet and came up with underwear, a baggy pair of jeans, a sweat-shirt with a dancing cow on the front and striped blue and green socks. "Here, try these on."

The jeans were too wide at the waist, but Laura cinched them in with a belt. She appraised Theo. "That'll do for now. Tomorrow morning I'll take you downtown and get you some clothes of your own. Here, try these old shoes of Anna's."

Theo slipped on a pair of dingy white runners. She wondered what had happened to her own clothes—the ones she'd been wearing and the ones packed in the duffel bag. And Sabrina, and the library book she had taken ... But that made her wonder about Rae again. She quickly pushed down any more thoughts of her life before today.

The cat emerged from under the bed and trotted over to Theo. It gave a short "Mrra!"

"I see you've already met Beardsley," Laura laughed.

"Doesn't Bingo chase him?" asked Theo.

"Oh, no, they're the best of friends. Sometimes they even sleep together."

Theo sighed with content. Even the dog and cat were perfect.

A door slammed downstairs. "Mum! Where are you! Where's Theo?"

Laura held out her hand. "Are you ready? Let's go down."

8

Theo sat quietly at the kitchen table while John, Anna, Lisbeth and Ben competed to tell her things.

"One at a time," Laura kept saying. "Let poor Theo have some peace!"

But Theo felt like a limp rag doll that was being passed around from hand to hand. She listened to Anna's story about her friend and assured John that she felt all right. She nodded when Lisbeth asked if she liked her room and while Ben told her more about his imaginary iguana.

"Grace was allowed to record a new message on their answering machine and do you know what she said, Theo? 'Please leave a message after the *honk*.' Her parents didn't notice until this morning and—"

"—Try one of these, Theo, they're—"

"—If you don't like the single bed you can have the lower bunk. And you can sleep with any of my animals or dolls you like, even Heather. She's my most favourite, I got her—"

"—Mortimer usually eats flies and bees, but sometimes he eats—"

"Everyone be *quiet!*" said Laura. They were for about half a minute and then they all started nattering again.

"You have really pretty hair, Theo. I wish I had curly hair. It's not fair that Ben got it."

"—and my soccer team is in the finals this Saturday—"

"—and sometimes Mortimer *bites* but I won't let him bite you—"

"I'm learning a really hard piece on the piano right now."

Theo turned her face to look at John. "That's nice," she whispered. She nibbled her sandwich again, but she wasn't hungry. She was full of breakfast and full of something else—this new melting sensation that filled her like soothing warm water.

"It's twenty to one," said Laura finally. "Off you go, you older ones. You can see Theo after school."

"It's not fair!" said Lisbeth. "Can't we stay home? Theo won't have anyone to play with."

"*I* can play with Theo. What about me?" demanded Ben.

"You'll be taking your nap. *Please*, Mum …"

"I want to stay home, too," said Anna. John nodded beside her.

Laura regarded them. "I do have a lot of phone calls to make and I don't want you to be lonely while Ben naps, Theo."

"I'm not *having* a nap," said Ben.

Laura ignored him. "Okay, one of you can stay home … Lisbeth."

"That's not fair!" said Anna. "Lisbeth always gets her own way!"

"Why can't we all stay?" said John.

"Just Lisbeth," said Laura firmly. "Theo needs to get used to you one at a time. All of you are too overwhelming."

"Lisbeth's the *most* overwhelming," complained Anna. She and John stomped out the door.

"Lisbeth, why don't you show Theo your guinea pig? Come on, Benny, let's have a story about Curious George before your nap."

"I don't *need* a nap!" said Ben, but he yawned as he followed his mother out of the kitchen.

Lisbeth looked ready to burst with importance. Theo was glad that Laura had picked her. She talked so much she was easy to be with.

The guinea pig, Snow White, lived in the laundry room. Lisbeth took her out of her cage and Snow White sniffed around the floor, making whistling noises. Lisbeth put her in Theo's hands. The guinea pig's claws tickled and she felt like a wriggly ball.

They went upstairs and Lisbeth introduced Theo to all her stuffed animals and dolls, then all of Anna's—each had a name. Theo chose Peppermint, a floppy pink cat, and a small owl called Hoot to put on her own bed.

"Are you sure you don't want Heather?" said Lisbeth, clutching the beautiful doll. She looked relieved when Theo shook her head.

Lisbeth let her hold Heather. "I got her for Christmas from Grannie and Gramps. Grannie knitted a whole lot of clothes for her."

She told Theo the names of all the people in her class. "I wish you were in grade two like me. Then I could be with you every minute!"

Laura peeked in. "Are you all right, Theo?"

"Yes … Mum." Theo blushed. She'd said it!

Laura—*Mum*—smiled at her. "I'll be working downstairs if you need me. Lisbeth, could you *please* try to tidy up this mess?"

Lisbeth picked up a few of the clothes and shoved them into the closet. She gave up quickly. "Most of this is Anna's stuff," she said. "I don't see why I should have to do all the work."

They played two games of Pizza Party, then made bead necklaces from a craft kit. "This is really Anna's," explained Lisbeth. "She never lets me touch it, but I don't think she'd mind if *you* used it. And of course I have to help you."

Lisbeth acted as if it were completely normal that Theo was part of the family. She didn't say anything about being on the ferry or wishing, and Theo was afraid to break the spell and ask about it. She listened to Lisbeth chatter and tried to believe that she was now her sister.

While Lisbeth was putting away the beads, Theo bent to look at the books. "Are all these yours?" she asked in wonder.

"Well, we all share them. John and Ben have lots more in their rooms." Lisbeth pulled out *Charlotte's Web*. "Do you want to hear me read?"

When Theo nodded, Lisbeth read the first page in a slow, careful stacatto, following the sentences with her finger. She let out her breath at the end. "There!" She looked expectant. "This is a hard book for grade two," she added.

Theo realized what she wanted. "You're a really good reader!" she told Lisbeth. The younger girl's face glowed like a small sun—as if Theo's praise really mattered.

She looks up to me! thought Theo. Like a big sister!

"I used to love this book," she said shyly. "Would you like me to read some more of it to you?"

"Sure!" They sat on Theo's bed and leaned against the wall. Theo began to read the familiar story. Ben wandered in, dressed only in a T-shirt and underpants. He curled up on one side of Theo, sucking his thumb. His plump body was warm and sticky and smelled like bread. Lisbeth pressed against her on the other side and then Bingo came in and settled on the floor.

Theo tried to make the farmyard world of Fern and Wilbur and Charlotte come alive for them. She looked up once to remind herself where she was. The last time she'd been immersed in this story she'd escaped to it in desperation—escaped from her scary school and the bleak shelter she and Rae were living in.

But look at her now! Sitting in a pleasantly cluttered room with a sister and brother on each side of her and a dog at her feet … This was too good to be real.

But it's not *real*, Theo reminded herself. It's *magic*.

"Read!" commanded Ben.

Theo smiled at him and continued the story.

By the time the others got home from school, it had stopped raining. As soon as they'd had a snack, they all went out.

Theo walked down the front steps of the house, rolling up the sleeves on the jacket Anna had lent her. The four Kaldors—five, counting Bingo—jostled and pressed around her. It was like being on the cover of *All-of-a-Kind Family*.

"What should we show her first?" asked John.

"The graveyard!" said Lisbeth. "Come on, Theo!" She grabbed Theo's hand and led her across the street. They went through an entrance in the holly hedge and into what looked like a large park. Huge trees spread their branches against the clearing sky. The grass was studded with gravestones, some upright and some flat; it looked like a grey and green chessboard.

"No one minds if we play in here," said Anna.

"Sometimes we play *ghosts*!" said Lisbeth. "I think this place is haunted, don't you Ben?"

Ben took Anna's hand. "Don't worry, there's no such thing as ghosts," she told him.

"Ben thinks there is. Last year he asked me if that was where the ghosts went to the bathroom!" Lisbeth pointed to a public washroom by the road.

"That was when I was *little*," said Ben.

They trekked over the wet grass, showing Theo their favourite graves—a black iron anchor, a fireman's hat, a stone eagle with outspread wings. There was a baby's chair with two tiny stone shoes on it and a bush clipped into the shape of an armchair. Some of the monuments were tall columns or huge vaults that John said were for rich families. Some of the gravestones were cracked or caked with moss or tilted in the grass.

"This cemetery is really old," John told Theo. "Dad told me lots of people from B.C. history are buried here, like Sir James Douglas and Emily Carr."

"They give tours sometimes," said Anna. "Once John and I tagged along and listened to the guide tell spooky stories about some of the dead people."

They had reached a tall stone angel with a gentle face. "This is our favourite place," said Anna. They sat on the steps circling the angel while Ben collected sticks.

A crow landed on a cross near them and rattled its throat. The sun appeared briefly and everything gleamed:

the freshly washed grass dotted with snowdrops, the red berries and yellow forsythia blossoms lighting up the shrubs. Beyond the cemetery was the sea. Theo hadn't realized the Kaldors lived so close to it.

She examined some graves near her. Some of the letters were so clogged with moss they were hard to read. Some just said "Mother" or "At Rest."

All of these people were *dead* ... It gave her a shivery feeling. She tried to avoid stepping on any of the stones.

"Snerd to the me-mor-y of ..." read Lisbeth carefully.

"Snerd!" Anna giggled. "*Sacred*, silly."

"I'm not silly!" said Lisbeth.

"No, you're not," said John. "Come on, let's show Theo the beach."

He led them out of another gate and down the hill until they reached a much busier street along the water. When John said it was safe, they dashed across the road and descended some concrete steps to a pebbly beach.

"Sometimes I fish here," John explained to Theo. "But I've never caught anything. Dad did—he caught an eight-pound salmon!"

"Fishing's so boring," said Anna. They walked along a breakwater for a while, throwing sticks for Bingo. He emerged from the water looking like a sleek black seal.

"Won't he get cold?" asked Theo, as Bingo galloped in again.

"He's a water dog," Ben told her. "He can swim in much colder water than this."

A group of ducks, some with ringed necks and striped heads, bobbed near them; John said they were called Harlequin ducks. He pointed across the sea. "The Olympic Mountains are over there, but it's too cloudy to see them today."

"We've been there," said Anna. "They're in the United States. Once we hiked up Hurricane Ridge and looked back at Victoria."

"I *hate* hiking," said Lisbeth.

"You're just lazy," said Anna. "Our family goes on lots of hikes, Theo. Lis pretends not to like it, but she does really. Sometimes we camp, too. You can share Lisbeth's and my tent, Theo."

Theo thought of the kids in *Swallows and Amazons*— they were always sleeping in tents. "That would be great," she said softly. "When do you go?"

"Usually in July," said John. "Dad said that this year we might go to Long Beach. You'll love it there, Theo. The beaches are huge!"

Theo still couldn't accept that they were including her so easily. So far no one had asked a thing about her former life—they just seemed eager to introduce her to her new one.

July was a long way off. She forced herself to believe

she would still be in this family then and take part in all these treats.

"I want to show Theo my mountain now," said Ben.

They trooped back across the busy road and up the steep street to their house. It backed onto what did look like a small mountain—a massive hill of rock with a low modern building on top.

The Kaldors climbed up easily, even Ben. Theo lagged behind until Anna came back and helped her find her footing on the mossy rocks.

"Sorry," she said. "I forgot you're not used to this like we are. We've been coming up here for three years, ever since we moved in."

They caught their breaths on a ledge beside the building. "That's a condominium," said John. "This part of the rock is their property, but they let us climb here."

Theo thought they'd reached the top, but then they went past the building and climbed even higher, pushing through bushes and along a muddy path to a towering part of the hill that looked out in all directions.

"Isn't this great?" panted John. He pointed out an island with a lighthouse, downtown Victoria and the Lieutenant-Governor's mansion. Gulls rose and fell from the water and a tug that looked like a toy boat plodded along the horizon. The sky was clearing and distant tips of mountains floated above the clouds. Theo could see the cemetery far below.

The Kaldors had their own park—the cemetery—their own beach, and their own mountain! Not really theirs—but it seemed so.

But now all these wonders belonged to Theo too! She feasted her eyes on the expanse of rock, water, trees and houses. She could come up here whenever she wanted and look again.

Then the sun streamed out of the sky in shimmering columns.

"Wow," said Anna.

"Do you like it, Theo?" said Lisbeth proudly, as if she had ordered the glowing scene herself.

"It's … beautiful," said Theo. So beautiful it hurt. She wished she could find a better word to express how the sun made purple-green canyons of the remaining clouds and how the silvery sea seemed to stretch on forever. She thought of the dreary streets and buildings she had always known and felt like Heidi coming to the Alps. "It's like magic," she whispered.

Then she couldn't help blurting out the question that kept nagging at her. "*Is* this magic?" she asked them. "Did I really come here because I wished on the moon?"

But none of them seemed to hear. "Let's go back," said John. "I have a music lesson at four-thirty."

"John's really good at piano," said Anna, as they made

their way down. "And I sing in a choir. What do you like to do, Theo?"

This was the first time anyone had asked about herself. "I don't know," said Theo.

"Maybe you could take ballet with me," said Lisbeth. "This year I'm going to be a bumble-bee in our spring concert."

"I don't like dancing," said Theo quickly.

"What about soccer?" said Anna. "My best friend, Grace, and I are on the same team. Do you want to try it?"

"Maybe," said Theo. "But I've never played soccer before."

"It's easy," said Anna. "You just run around and try to kick the ball whenever it comes near you."

When they reached their backyard, John left on his bike for his lesson and Anna went in to do her homework. Lisbeth and Ben showed Theo how to climb a tree that towered over the house.

She'd never climbed a tree before. Ben scrambled to the top like a monkey, while Theo perched shakily on a branch. She touched its strange, peeling bark.

"What kind of a tree is this?" she asked them.

"An arbutus," said Lisbeth. "There are lots of them here. Grannie tried to grow one in Vancouver but it died."

"Arbutus," said Theo carefully. She stored the word in her packed mind, along with Emily Carr, Olympic

Mountains and Harlequin ducks. She pressed her cheek against the smooth orange trunk of the tree. Even it seemed to welcome her.

THE EVENING was as full of delights as the day had been. Theo, Lisbeth and Ben were watching TV when they heard a whistle—two high notes and a low one.

"Daddy!" shouted Ben, running into the hall. Lisbeth dashed after him and Theo followed slowly, recalling his name—Dan.

Bingo hurtled into the hall and threw himself at Dan, his mouth slack with worship—as if he were saying, "I love all of you very much but this is my *master*!"

"Hello there, Theo," said Dan, hanging up his raincoat. Theo hung her head; she didn't know what you were supposed to say to fathers. She remembered that she'd told Mum she'd call him "Dad," but maybe Dan didn't know that yet.

The whole family congregated in the kitchen, the adults trying to put together dinner while the children got in the way. When they were finally sitting down, Dan turned to Theo and said, "Laura phoned and told me you wanted to call us Mum and Dad, Theo. I'm so pleased."

He had such a comfortable voice and his eyes twinkled behind their glasses. Theo shyly returned his smile and gulped down delicious mouthfuls of pasta.

After dinner Theo sat in the living-room and watched Dan—*Dad*—carefully start a fire with newspaper and kindling.

"We're only allowed to watch two TV programs a day," said Lisbeth. "It's so unfair!"

Theo thought it was peaceful. Everyone sat in the large, cluttered room doing something. Mum and Dad read the paper, John did his math homework, Anna read a book, Ben played with Lego, and Lisbeth lay on her stomach, drawing pictures of guinea pigs wearing clothes. Theo sat down beside Ben and helped him build a castle. But she kept lifting her head and gazing at the family. They still seemed too perfect to be real.

At seven-thirty Dad took Ben upstairs to give him a bath. Theo joined the others around the dining-room table for a game of Monopoly. Then Mum looked at her watch and said, "Bedtime, girls."

"Not *yet*," complained Lisbeth. But she led Theo and Anna up the stairs and they got into their pyjamas and brushed their teeth. Dad came up and sat on Theo's bed while they settled on each side of him. He was holding a book with a worn leather cover.

"I thought we'd start something new tonight, in honour of Theo," he said. He opened up the book. "This is a story by a man called Rudyard Kipling. It's called 'The Cat That Walked by Himself.'"

His deep voice began: "'Hear and attend and listen; for this befell and behappened and became and was, O my Best Beloved, when the Tame animals were wild.'"

It was the most wonderful story Theo had ever heard—eery and enchanting and completely satisfying.

"'... when the moon gets up and night comes, he is the Cat that walks by himself, and all places are alike to him. Then he goes out to the Wet Wild Woods or up the Wet Wild Trees or on the Wet Wild Roofs, waving his wild tail and walking by his wild lone,'" finished Dad.

Beardsley, who had been lying in Lisbeth's lap, stood up and stalked out of the room with his tail straight up in the air. They all laughed.

"He was listening!" said Lisbeth. "But Bingo's not a proper dog, Daddy, because he never chases Beardsley."

"Bingo doesn't know he's a dog," said Dad. "He thinks he's a person. Time for bed, now."

He tucked each of them in and kissed them. His beard tickled.

A few minutes later Mum came up and kissed them too. "Anna's allowed to read for half an hour," she said. "You can too, Theo."

"I'm too sleepy to read," said Theo.

"Good night, then," said Mum. "I'm so glad you've come to us."

Theo was half-awake when Anna turned out her light.

"Are you okay?" she asked. "Do you want a drink of water or anything?"

"I'm okay."

"Good night, then. See you in the morning."

"Good night," whispered Theo.

She wriggled further into her pink flannel nest, hugging Peppermint and Hoot. She had a flash of longing for Sabrina, but she closed her eyes against any thoughts of her real life. The perfect day was over.

9

Theo was afraid to open her eyes the next morning. She was sure she'd be back on the ferry, waking up after the most incredible dream of her life. But she heard someone thump out of the upper bunk. Then Anna was bouncing on Theo's feet. "Good morning!" She grinned. "I can't believe you're really here!"

"Neither can I," said Theo, grinning just as wide.

Lisbeth threw her pillow at them and they started a wild fight until Dad stuck his head in and told them to get dressed.

"Can't Theo go to school with us today?" asked Lisbeth at breakfast.

"No, I want to take her shopping for clothes," said Mum.

"Can I come?" cried Lisbeth and Anna at the same time.

Mum shook her head. "It would be too hard to concentrate with you two along. If she feels like it, she can go to school with you tomorrow. What do you think, Theo?"

"Maybe," whispered Theo, because the girls looked so eager. But she didn't want to go to school—this blissful bubble might burst.

Ben had gone with Dad and the other children left too. Then Mum and Theo got into the van and drove to a mall. Mum was a swift, efficient shopper. They whisked in and out of several stores where she bought Theo more clothes than she'd ever owned in her life.

Jeans, T-shirts, leggings with tunic tops, sweaters … purple runners, black party shoes, yellow gum boots … a hooded raincoat, a blue fleecy jacket like Anna's … pastel underwear, dozens of colourful socks, several pairs of tights … a bathing suit, pyjamas, a nightgown and a housecoat … and a beautiful purple flowered dress that came with a matching headband.

"There!" said Mum. "With these and Anna's hand-me-downs you should be set until summer. I hope you don't mind that some of your clothes are secondhand, Theo."

Theo was speechless. When they got home, she helped Mum cut off the price tags and hang up the new clothes, plus some that used to belong to Anna, in the space Mum had cleared for her in the closet. Dad had brought up a little dresser just for her. Theo lovingly placed her underwear, T-shirts and sweaters in it.

"I've hardly ever had *new* clothes," she said.

Mum looked surprised. "Well, it's about time you did. Why don't you change out of those baggy jeans and put on something of your own? The others will be home soon."

Theo took a long time deciding. Finally she picked purple leggings, a purple and yellow top and yellow socks. She tied up the brand new laces on her brand new runners.

The second pair of new shoes she'd had this year! She remembered the ones Rae had bought her.

"Mum ..." she said slowly. "Where's—where's my *real* mother? Where's Rae?"

Then she wished she hadn't asked. But she didn't need to worry. Laura kept her back to Theo as she continued to hang up clothes. She either hadn't heard or didn't want to answer.

"Theo! You look wonderful!" said Anna, as she and Lisbeth burst into the room. They examined all the new clothes. Anna brushed back Theo's hair and secured it with two purple barrettes. "There—you're perfect!"

"You're *beautiful*, Theo," said Lisbeth. She gazed at Theo the way Bingo gazed at Dad.

After lunch Mum took Theo out again, this time to get her hair cut. "What lovely thick curls!" said the hairdresser. When she'd finished, Theo's hair stood out around her face in a soft dark circle. She gazed at the smiling purple and yellow girl in the mirror and felt more than ever that this must be magic.

WHEN THEY GOT BACK, Mum showed Theo her studio. The small room was crammed with jars of pencils and paints, wide shallow drawers full of paper, and more felt pens than Theo had ever seen at one time. Drawings were pinned all over the walls, of cartoony children playing or animals in clothes. Some of the children looked like the Kaldors.

"Did you do all these?" asked Theo in awe.

Laura nodded. "Here, I'll draw something for you." She took out a square of paper and a black pen. Like magic she sketched a picture of Beardsley curled in a ball and handed it to Theo.

"To *keep*?"

"Of course!" said Mum. "Would you like to draw something while I finish this card?"

She sat Theo down at a little table beside a wide sloping desk. "Each of the children has drawn here while I work, although none of them could sit for long. John was the most patient, but Ben's impossible—he doesn't last more than five minutes."

Theo gazed at the creamy piece of paper in front of her—it seemed too good to mark. She thought a moment, then picked up an orange felt pen and began to draw the arbutus tree in the backyard. It was fun to add brown for the peeling bark and different greens for the leaves.

"That's wonderful, Theo!" said Mum. "You've really *looked* at that tree!"

"You can keep it," whispered Theo.

"Thank you! Did you sign it?" Theo wrote her name in the lower right corner, where Mum had in her picture of Beardsley. Then Mum pinned it over her desk.

"I need to finish this design today," she said. "Will you be all right playing on your own until the others get home?"

Theo nodded; she longed to explore. First she took Mum's drawing and taped it to the wall beside her bed. Then she began to go over every inch of the house. If this did turn out to be a dream, she wanted to remember it forever.

She had never seen as much luxury. Bedrooms with beds covered in soft quilts, and full of toys, games and clothes. Two bathrooms with soft fluffy towels and many bottles of shampoo and lotions. Four telephones! Soft chairs, rugs and pretty pictures on the walls, tables piled with magazines, a piano. Not only a TV, but a VCR, a stereo, a CD player and a computer. A washer and dryer, an iron, a toaster, a blender, a microwave and dozens of dishes. In the basement she found bicycles, skis, skate-boards, skates with blades and skates with wheels, and a toboggan. And everywhere, shelves and shelves of books.

The house was warm and clean and although some of the furniture was shabby, it wasn't broken. Theo hadn't spotted a mouse or a cockroach since she'd been here. The refrigerator and cupboards were crammed with food. The van was parked in the driveway and Dad had driven a smaller car to work.

"You must be very rich!" Theo told Mum back in the studio.

"Rich?" Mum laughed. "We've never thought of ourselves as rich! We have a large mortgage and it's a real struggle to pay for things like John's music lessons and Anna's braces. The cars are both getting old but we can't afford a new one, and we really need to add another room."

"But you have so much!" said Theo.

Mum looked at her. "Yes," she said quietly. "We have so much. We're very, very lucky." She gave Theo a hug. "And now we have you, too."

Theo shook her head when Mum asked her if she wanted to go to school the next morning. Mum said gently, "You're just not ready, are you? I'll tell you what— you can stay home for the rest of this week if you try to be brave enough to go on Monday—is it a deal?"

Theo nodded. Maybe she wouldn't be here next week. Maybe the dream would end by then.

She had now decided that being here was a dream. In the books she'd read magic had always made sense; it was never as simple as just wishing on the new moon. She'd probably fallen asleep on the ferry and *dreamt* she'd wished.

If she had come here by magic, there would be an explanation. Anna or Lisbeth would say, "Isn't it wonderful that your wish came true?" But no one had said that. No one asked Theo any questions or referred to her past or thought that it was in any way odd that she was here. And the two times she'd asked them they didn't seem to hear. It *didn't* make sense—so it must be a dream.

And only in a dream could anyone be as happy as she felt. Only in a dream could everything be so easy. She didn't have to do anything. She was simply *here*—bathed in love and acceptance, soaking up this wonderful family and their safe and comfortable life.

Theo floated through the rest of the week, trying not to think about waking up. Sometimes she watched Mum work, or she read or she played with Beardsley, trailing a bit of string for him to attack. Often she just lay dozily on the living-room couch, watching the birds at the feeder outside the window. The morning silence was broken by the noisy arrival of the others home for lunch. Theo sat passively and soaked up the stories they told her.

In the afternoons, after Ben woke up from his nap, Theo took him and Bingo for a walk—although it felt as though they were taking her. Sometimes they climbed up the mountain, and sometimes they explored the cemetery; Mum said they weren't to go to the beach without the others. Theo held Ben's hand as they crossed the street, just like a big sister.

Ben often made Theo attach Bingo's leash to his belt loop so he could be a horse that she ordered to walk or trot or gallop. Or he wanted her to be his partner in a game—another pirate or another warrior. It was relaxing to act like a four-year-old.

"When I was little, I pretended I was a fairy," she told him.

"A fairy!" scoffed Ben. "I'm a *knight*! You can be my squire, okay? Bingo's a dragon." They galloped along the path in the cemetery after Bingo, Ben waving his plastic sword.

After school they returned to the cemetery with Anna and Lisbeth. Then they played hide-and-seek, crouching behind the vaults or bushes or trees and trying not to shout "Home Free!" too loud. But whenever they passed a cemetery gardener, he just smiled at them.

They always ended up resting at the foot of their favourite angel. On Friday afternoon John found them there on his way home from his friend's. Theo edged closer to him as he sat down. John didn't usually play with them—he was in grade seven, after all. *He* was like a knight, thought Theo—gentle and kind and brave. Yesterday he had picked up a garter snake in the yard and put it back in the bushes.

They watched some men near them dig a deep hole. "I bet someone's going to be buried there!" said Lisbeth.

"That's unusual," said John. "Dad said most of the spaces in this cemetery are taken up."

"Imagine being put under the ground and staying there forever and forever," shuddered Anna.

"You wouldn't know," said John. "You'd be dead."

"Well, imagine being *dead*. Not being able to see or hear or breathe." Anna turned her back on the hole.

"Being dead is just like having a long sleep," said Lisbeth. "That's what Mummy said when Grandpa died."

"No it isn't—you turn into an angel, like that one," said Ben, pointing up to the statue. "Peter's grandma is an angel." Peter was his best friend.

"But what if you weren't ready to die?" said Anna. "What if you weren't old like Grandpa was? And you had to go into the cold ground and stay there!"

"If I wasn't ready to die, I wouldn't stay there," said John. "I'd come back."

"You mean you'd be a ghost?" said Lisbeth. She moved closer to Anna. "You shouldn't talk that way, John. You're scaring Ben."

Theo felt scared too. She looked at the gaping hole and the gravestones surrounding them. She was glad when they talked about this weekend instead.

THAT EVENING they piled into the van and drove to Chinatown for dinner. Theo ate sweet-and-sour spare-ribs and almond chicken for the first time. John and

Anna and Mum and Dad were the only ones who could manage chopsticks. Then they went to a video store and after a long argument decided on one video for the children and one for the adults.

Theo curled up between Anna and Mum on the couch in the den, weeping with them over the ending of *Old Yeller*. Even Dad was sniffing.

"What babies!" said John.

"You cried, too," said Anna. "I saw you wipe your eyes on the cushion."

"Why did that doggie have to die, Mummy?" asked Ben tearfully.

"It's only a story, Benny," said Mum, pulling him onto her lap. She blew her nose. "Oh, dear, it was even worse than I remembered."

"Sometimes it's nice to cry, isn't it?" said Lisbeth after they were in bed.

Not usually, thought Theo, remembering the evening before she and Rae had left Vancouver. But tonight she had indulged in a sadness that wasn't real—that was just a story.

On saturday John had a karate class, Lisbeth and Ben had swimming lessons, and Theo went to watch Anna's soccer game. Anna was a good player—she ran fast and scored several goals. It looked like fun.

After the game Anna introduced Theo to her best

friend. "This is Grace Leung. Grace, this is my new sister, Theo."

Her new sister! Theo felt herself melt again. "Hi," she whispered.

"It's good to meet you, Theo," said Grace. She had a friendly smile.

The three of them walked home together. On the way they stopped at a store to spend their allowance. Dad had given Theo a two-dollar coin that morning.

Two whole dollars! Theo picked out candy like the others. She thought of how shocked Anna and Grace would be if they knew she used to steal it. But today she handed her money proudly to the clerk.

After lunch the whole family went to Thetis Lake for a hike. Bingo went berserk, rushing down to the water and coming back soaked. The dark green lake was fringed by firs and rocks. They climbed a high path and looked over all of it.

That evening Mum and Dad visited some friends, Anna went to Grace's for a sleepover and John babysat.

"Go to bed!" he ordered Lisbeth and Ben and Theo, long after nine o'clock. They were huddled in the den, wolfing down popcorn and watching a scary movie called *The Birds*.

"No," said Lisbeth.

"We don't want to," said Ben. He was straddling the arm of the couch, pretending it was a horse.

"You're supposed to do as I say," grumbled John. "All the other kids I babysit do."

"They don't know what you're really like," said Lisbeth. "They don't know that you still keep your teddy bear on your bed."

John lunged at her, picked her up and carried her screaming to her room. By the time he had returned for Ben, Lisbeth had dashed downstairs again. Ben ran into the kitchen and John turned to Theo.

"Come on," he pleaded. "Bed."

"Okay," said Theo, getting up.

"No, Theo!" cried Lisbeth. "Run away!"

Theo looked at John. She didn't want to hurt his feelings. But then she noticed how he was trying not to laugh. "Go to bed, both of you!" he repeated.

Theo hesitated—then shook her head with a grin and shot into the living-room. John caught her by an arm and a leg and tried to drag her across the hall. Ben scampered in and he and Lisbeth flung themselves on top of John. They thrashed in a giggling pile while Bingo barked around them.

Theo laughed so much her insides became hollowed out and her belly ached. They all lay on the floor, helpless and limp.

"I give up," gasped John. "Stay up as late as you want, but don't blame me if you get into trouble. I should be paid triple for looking after you guys!"

He went into the kichen and made more popcorn. They collapsed in front of the TV again. Ben soon fell asleep and John carried him upstairs. Then Lisbeth's eyes began to close and John helped her to bed, Theo trailing behind. When she finally closed her eyes she gave one last, delighted giggle.

ON SUNDAY all the Kaldors got out their bikes. They offered Theo an old one of Anna's to ride but she shook her head. "I don't know how," she whispered.

"You don't know how to ride a two-wheeler?" said Lisbeth in astonishment. "I learned when I was five! Even Ben can ride one with training wheels."

"Be quiet, Lisbeth," said John. "Don't worry, Theo—I'll teach you."

Theo followed him into the cemetery. John held the small bicycle upright while Theo climbed on. It felt dangerously tippy, but she wanted to please him.

"Okay, now I'm going to hold the saddle," said John. "Go!"

Theo pushed the pedals harder and harder while John ran behind. The bike wobbled a bit but she kept her balance.

"Good!" puffed John. He stopped the bike and showed Theo how to use the brakes. "Okay, let's try again—this time I'm going to let you go."

"I'll fall!" said Theo.

"No, you won't—you'll be fine. Just brake when you want to stop." Theo wanted to protest further but John's enthusiasm was very strong. He *believed* in her.

"Ready?" Theo gulped, then nodded. John held onto the seat as she pedalled—then he let go.

She rode steadily for a few minutes, then started to wobble. But she squeezed the brakes and the bike came to an obedient halt. She'd done it!

John ran up. "Good for you!" Both of them were bursting with pride.

Theo practised turning, braking and getting on and off. After an hour she could do it all—she could ride a bike!

THAT EVENING some relatives came for dinner—Mum's mother, Dad's brother and sister-in-law, and three small cousins—a baby called Emma, a two-year-old boy called Sam, and Linnea, who was a year older than Ben.

The grown-ups talked and laughed in the living-room while the eight children interrupted. Everyone smiled at Theo and welcomed her to the family. Lisbeth hauled around the baby and Sam shadowed Ben.

All the children ate at the kitchen table while Emma banged her spoon in a highchair beside it. Theo smoothed her new purple dress over her knees, her mouth watering at the plate of roast chicken and mashed potatoes an adult put in front of her.

"Now we're *eight* cousins!" said Anna, cutting up Sam's meat. "There's a book called that."

"Cheers!" cried Linnea, clinking her glass of ginger ale against Ben's.

Theo looked around the happy circle of chewing, noisy faces. She melted into it and tried not to think of school tomorrow.

10

"Are you ready, Theo?" said Mum. "I've told the school you're coming. Anna will take you to Ms. Tremblay's class."

Theo tried to feel ready, but she shivered inside with the same dread she always felt at starting another school. She'd put on her new plaid pants, with a matching green top and red vest. The Kaldors kept telling her how nice the teachers and kids were. Theo tried to remember all the times in books when someone had started a new school and discovered it was fine. But it had never been fine for her.

It wasn't fair! she thought, as she walked the few blocks with John and Anna and Lisbeth. So far this dream had been perfect. Now it could turn into a nightmare.

But she'd forgotten that she wasn't alone any more— she belonged to a real family. Every time the Kaldors saw a friend, they introduced Theo as their new sister; every time, the other person gave Theo a welcoming smile.

When they crossed a busy street and reached the playground of a high brick school, John went over to join some older boys. Anna, Lisbeth and Theo were immediately surrounded by an excited group of girls. All Theo had to do was stand and listen.

A buzzer sounded. "Come on, Theo, I'll take you to your classroom," said Anna.

"See you at recess!" called Lisbeth.

Theo's stomach lurched. But a pleasant-looking teacher greeted them at the door of the grade-four classroom. "So this is Theo! I've heard so much about you. I hope you'll be very happy here."

Anna went off to the grade-five room; it was scary to say goodbye to her. Ms. Tremblay led Theo to a table and introduced her to the three students who would be sharing it with her: Jasmin, Will and Elise. They greeted her warmly.

But this had happened every time Theo had started a new school. The other kids always *began* by being friendly.

Today, however, they didn't act as if they felt sorry for her. They didn't have to! She was clean and rested and well fed, dressed in crisp new clothes, and armoured with the love of her new family.

"You're John's sister, aren't you?" said Will. "My brother's his best friend."

"I like your vest," said Elise.

"Did anyone watch *The Birds* on Saturday night?" asked Jasmin.

"I did," said Will. "My parents were out so my brother and I saw the whole thing."

Theo took a deep breath. "So did I. Wasn't it scary?"

"You must be really brave," said Elise. "I can't watch movies like that."

Ms. Tremblay began telling them about South Africa. Theo tried to pay attention. To her surprise, it wasn't as hard to do so as usual. Later in the morning Ms. Tremblay asked Theo to name some of the books she'd read. She looked surprised when Theo reeled off a long list.

"What a wonderful reader!" she said. "We like books in this class, Theo. I think you're going to feel right at home." She asked Theo, Elise, Stefan and Yuko to draw a map based on the Narnia book the class had just finished. Theo found the others easy to talk to as they lay on the floor with their pencils and felts. She giggled with them when they were interrupted by a visit from Snuggles, the kindergarten rabbit who ran loose in the school.

"Is it okay?" Anna and Lisbeth asked her at recess. "Do you like our school?"

"It's great!" said Theo. In fact, it was so pleasant it didn't seem like school at all. The rest of the day passed just as smoothly as the morning.

THAT AFTERNOON Theo went for a long bike ride with Anna and Grace. She pedalled carefully as they rode along Dallas Road, on a sidewalk that edged a cliff overlooking the sea. She'd already walked along here on Sunday afternoons with the whole family.

"I think we should turn back now," said Anna, when they reached Government Street.

"Let's go downtown first," suggested Grace.

"I'm not allowed to go there without an adult," said Anna.

"Neither am I," said Grace, "but who's going to know? Come on, we can show Theo the Empress Hotel."

Anna looked reluctant, but she finally agreed. Theo followed them along a busy street to an enormous hotel that looked like a castle. They stopped by a stone wall and watched the boats in the harbour. Then they walked their bikes along the sidewalk, looking in the windows of the stores selling sweaters and china and souvenirs of Victoria. They paused to sniff deeply in the doorway of a chocolate shop.

"Let's go into the Eaton Centre," said Grace. "I need to pee."

"But what about our bikes?" said Anna.

"We can lock them here," said Grace, pointing to a railing.

"But I don't have a lock!" said Anna. "I lent it to John after his broke."

Grace looked impatient. "Well, you stay here and watch the bikes while Theo and I go in."

"I need to pee, too!" said Anna.

"I'll stay with the bikes," offered Theo.

"I don't want to leave you alone," said Anna. She looked at the bikes and at her friend's expression. "Okay … let's go in just for a minute so we can use the washroom. I'll lock my bike with Theo's. But we can't stay long—it's getting late."

Grace locked her bike to the railing. Anna wound the chain lock from Theo's bike around hers as well.

They went into Eaton's and used the washroom. Then Grace wanted to try on make-up.

"We really should go now, Grace," said Anna.

"Just a few more minutes," said Grace, spraying herself with a perfume sample.

When they finally went out again, Anna's bike was gone.

"Oh, no!" She knelt to examine the lock; the chain had been cut. "My brand new bike!" she wailed. "I just got it for Christmas!"

"That's why they picked yours," said Grace. "Don't cry. It's all my fault—I shouldn't have stayed so long. I'm sorry, Anna."

She put her arm around her friend, but Anna just cried harder. Then she sniffed, looked miserably at the others, and said, "There's nothing we can do. It's really late. We've got to get home! Let's go up Fairfield Road, it's faster."

Anna tried riding double with Grace, but they couldn't balance the bike and soon gave up. When they reached Fairfield, they pushed the bikes up the hilly street as fast as they could. Now it was dark—the streetlights were on and people pulled their curtains in the houses they passed. Without the sun the air was clammy.

Anna was close to tears again. "We're going to get into a lot of trouble," she told Theo. "Especially me!"

"So am I," said Grace gloomily. "I'm sorry, you guys. It was a dumb idea to go downtown."

Theo shuddered. What did "a lot of trouble" mean? "Anna," she asked, after they had said goodbye to Grace at her corner and hurried down their own street. "Are they going to hit us?"

Anna stopped in astonishment. "Hit us? Of course not! Mum and Dad would *never* hit us! It's wrong to hit children!"

"Oh." Theo was relieved, but she still trembled when they opened the front door.

"They're back!" shouted Lisbeth. "We thought you'd been kidnapped!"

Ben pushed into their stomachs with his hard head and Bingo licked their faces frantically.

"Anna! Theo!" cried Mum, rushing into the hall.

She put her arms around both of them at once. "Thank goodness you're safe!" Then she stepped back, her voice stern. "Where on *earth* have you been? Dad's gone out in the car to look for you. Do you realize what time it is?"

Dad burst in and hugged them violently. Then they all sat down in the living-room while Anna tried to explain. "It's not Theo's fault," she said at once. "It was Grace's idea, but I could have said no. And now I've lost my bike!" She began to cry again.

"But why didn't you phone us when you realized it was so late?" demanded Mum.

Anna hung her head. "I didn't think of that," she whispered.

"I'll contact the police about your bike," said Dad, "but I don't think there's much chance of getting it back. Now Anna …" He pulled her close to him. "You've been very foolish, haven't you … I'm sorry your new bike has been stolen, but I think you know it was your fault. You'll just have to make do with John's old one."

"We were so worried!" said Mum. Her anger had evaporated and tears slid down her face. She pulled Theo onto her lap.

"I'm s-sorry," sobbed Anna.

"I'm sorry," echoed Theo.

"Oh, come and have your dinner." Mum wiped her eyes. "I've kept it warm."

That night, after they were all in bed and after they'd gone over the whole afternoon in detail for Lisbeth, Theo whispered, "Anna?"

"What?"

"When are we going to get into trouble?"

Anna sounded puzzled. "What do you mean?"

"You said we'd get into a lot of trouble, but nothing's happened to us yet."

"Nothing! But they were so upset and Mum was crying! That was the trouble! I feel so terrible when they're disappointed in me! And I lost my *bike*. This has been the worst day of my life!" Anna's voice changed to quiet sobs ... then she fell asleep.

That was all? A lot of talking, ending with hugs and a hot dinner?

Theo felt sorry for Anna, but she had another bike to use, after all. The "worst day" ... if this was as bad as a day in this family could be, then as long as she remained in this dream nothing would ever be awful again.

Then Theo thought of the care and the worry in Mum and Dad's voices. They had worried about her as much as Anna. She was important to them. She really mattered ...

11

Spring unfolded in a succession of perfect, peaceful days. Theo learned how to play soccer and ride on a skateboard. She played the part of the dormouse in their class production of *Alice's Adventures in Wonderland*. She helped Lisbeth with her science project on earthworms and taught Ben how to tie his shoelaces.

During Spring Break the whole family went skiing at Mt. Washington. Theo had never seen so much snow. They fitted her out with Anna's old skis and boots. Even Ben was better than she was, but she didn't care. It was so exhilarating to career down the hill—tumbling into the soft snow, then struggling to her feet to whiz on.

On the first Saturday in April Anna turned eleven. She shrieked when she came downstairs to find a new bike with a ribbon on it in the hall. "Oh, thank you, *thank* you!" she cried, hugging her parents.

"There's a very good lock on it," said Dad. "Use it!"

Anna flushed. "I will," she promised.

Theo watched her unwrap the silver pendant of a dolphin she'd saved two allowances to buy. "It's beautiful!" said Anna, squeezing Theo hard.

That afternoon Mum took Anna, four of her friends, Theo and Lisbeth swimming. Theo had been taking lessons—she was in the same class as Lisbeth.

"Good, Theo!" called Lisbeth, after Theo jumped off the low board and splashed to the side. "I did that when I was six," she added. "But of course, you're still catching up."

Theo wasn't sure about swimming. She always felt cold and it was a struggle to keep from sinking. But the others were so encouraging she tried to like it.

After swimming they went back and sat around the dining-room table while Mum and Dad served them the meal Dad had prepared. Anna had ordered her favourites—lamb, roast potatoes and peas. The girls giggled as Dad acted like a waiter. "Would you care for a Coke, madam?"

Lisbeth was unusually quiet, thrilled at being allowed to stay instead of going with John and Ben to their cousins. "When's *your* birthday, Theo?" she whispered.

"June the twenty-sixth," said Theo. She'd be ten then. But would she still be here?

She was back to thinking that living with the Kaldors was magic—the visit had lasted too long for a dream. Maybe her wish *had* come true.

It didn't make sense that no one asked her a thing about her former life, that the Kaldors and even her teacher and new friends didn't seem to find it strange that she was here. But maybe one day she'd find out why she'd been whisked so easily into this happiness.

Sometimes Theo would lie awake and think of her mother. How had Rae felt when Theo had disappeared? Did she miss her? But thoughts like these made Theo squirm. It was easier to simply shut Rae and her former life out of her mind. The longer she lived with the family, the easier it became to forget that difficult time.

Living in Vancouver had been like swimming—always struggling to stay afloat. But living here was like skiing, flying down the hill with joy. She soared through each day, busy and relaxed and, best of all, cherished. Every morning she woke up with delight that she was still here. Her magic wish had come true. In fact, every wish she'd ever had seemed to have come true. It was like being in a story, even if the story wasn't logical. Her life was perfect.

Until the day the magic began to go wrong.

IT WAS A GLORIOUS APRIL afternoon. Theo and Anna and Lisbeth were lying on their backs under the angel. Above them towered trees dotted with new leaves and faded pink blossoms. More blossoms floated in the air like snowflakes.

Anna and Lisbeth were talking about this Easter

weekend, when the family was going to Vancouver to stay with Dad's parents. "You'll love it there, Theo," said Anna. "Their house is near the beach. Grannie is a potter. Sometimes she lets us try throwing pots on her wheel."

"And Gramps lets us ride on his golf cart," said Lisbeth.

Theo rolled to her stomach and pulled little white daisies out of the grass. She didn't want to go to Vancouver—what if she ran into Rae? Maybe being there again would undo the magic. Her head ached with confusion.

To her relief the other two stopped discussing it. They lay still in a dreamy silence. Theo sat up and gazed at the colourful plots around her; some were planted with tulips and grape hyacinths. The fragrant air caressed her and she tried to stop worrying. Maybe it would be all right; surely her new family would keep her safe, even in Vancouver.

She remembered she was supposed to take some sand to school tomorrow, for a shoebox diorama she and Jasmin were making. "I need to go to the beach," she said. "Want to come?"

The other two didn't answer. Had they fallen asleep?

But Anna's eyes were open and Lisbeth was humming, her hands in the air trying to catch falling blossoms. "I said, I'm going to the beach," said Theo more loudly.

They ignored her. A chill gripped Theo. "Anna!" she cried. Anna continued to stare at the sky. Theo jumped up. *"Anna! Lisbeth!"*

Anna sat up slowly, as if Theo had whispered, not shouted. "Did you say something?"

"Do you want to go to the beach?" croaked Theo.

"The beach?" Anna peered at Theo as if trying to put her into focus. "Sure! Come on, Lisbeth."

Lisbeth stood up and gave Theo the same puzzled stare. Then she took her hand. "Let's go." She held onto Theo all the way and Theo tried to forget what had happened.

BUT IT HAPPENED AGAIN. That night at dinner she asked John three times to pass the bread; he didn't seem to hear her. After dinner Ben sat right on top of her while she was reading.

"Ow!" cried Theo.

"Oh, it's you!" said Ben in a surprised voice. "I didn't see you."

Didn't *see* her? How could he not see her?

Over the next few days it got worse and worse. Sometimes the family would have a long conversation without including Theo. In school Ms. Tremblay stopped asking her questions. Theo spent whole recesses standing alone while the other kids ignored her, the way they had in her previous schools.

What was happening? If Theo was forceful—if she shouted or clutched at someone—she could usually get her family or teacher or friends to notice her again. But they always did so in a slightly puzzled way, as if it took them a minute to remember she was there.

Theo became more and more frightened. On Thursday she woke up with a pounding headache. At breakfast she said she was sick and didn't want to go to school. She repeated it twice before Mum said, "You go back to bed, then. I'll come and check on you when the others have left."

Theo huddled under her quilt and waited for a long time. Finally she stumbled to the head of the stairs. "Mum!" She had to call many more times before Mum appeared.

"What is it? Oh, *Theo*! I'm sorry, I'd forgotten you stayed home this morning."

Forgotten? Theo sat down on the stairs and exploded in tears.

"What's wrong, Theo?" Mum came up and led her back to bed, then sat down on the end of it.

"You're—you're *all* forgetting me!" sobbed Theo. "All this week everyone keeps ignoring me! As if—as if I don't *exist*!"

"Now, Theo, that's nonsense. You're imagining things because you don't feel well." Mum smoothed the quilt around her and gave her a kiss. "We'd never ignore you. You're one of us now! We love you! I'm going to bring you up some ginger ale, okay? I'll be right back."

Theo tried to stop crying. That must be it. It must be

feeling sick that made her feel so—so *invisible*. Mum's reassuring words calmed her. She waited for her to return.

She waited and waited but Mum forgot to come back.

Finally Theo crept downstairs. Mum's back was to her, concentrating on a painting. Theo stamped her feet and Bingo looked up from his cushion with surprise, but Mum didn't budge.

Theo opened the refrigerator door and got some ginger ale herself. She carried the glass upstairs, drank it quickly, then hid her head under the quilt and sobbed until she fell asleep.

WHEN THE OTHERS CAME home for lunch, Theo found she had disappeared for good. She stood in the kitchen in her pyjamas and yelled until she was hoarse. "John! Anna and Lisbeth! Ben! Mum!" But now even Bingo and Beardsley ignored her.

Theo pulled at Lisbeth's dress, thumped John's back, and tried to pick up Ben. They all carried on eating their sandwiches and talking to each other.

"*Please*," begged Theo. "It's me. I'm your sister! I *belong* to you!"

They didn't hear her. Theo's throbbing head felt as if it were about to burst. The kitchen whirled; she swayed to keep her balance, then fell to the floor. She closed her eyes and all was darkness.

PART 3

Cecily

12

She opened her eyes to a blur of people and chairs and windows.

"No!" whispered Theo, shaking her head frantically. But she couldn't shake away the scene before her. She was back on the ferry.

Nothing had changed since she'd been sitting here with Rae. The teenager beside her was still opening his bag of chips. The peculiar-looking woman who had been standing by the window was back. She was still staring at Theo but then she walked away, giving Theo a last, yearning glance before she left.

I don't want to be *here*! thought Theo. But she was. That meant it must have been a dream after all—not magic. The long, blissful months she'd belonged to a real family hadn't happened. At least the awful time at the end hadn't happened either; but being back here was worse.

"What's eating *you*? You look strange." Rae had slipped into her seat again.

"Where were you?" Theo asked in bewilderment.

"Out on the deck having a smoke, of course. I told you that—have you been asleep?"

"Did you see any kids out there?"

"Yeah, some. Why?"

"Did you see four in one family? Two boys and two girls?"

"I didn't look at anyone closely. Who are you talking about?"

Theo forgot to be careful. "The Kaldors!" she said. "John and Anna and Lisbeth and Ben! We were playing on the deck, pretending to fly. They were really nice."

"On the deck?" Rae leaned forward and gripped Theo's arm. "Did you go outside after I told you to stay here?"

"No—I—I didn't really. Could you let go?"

Rae relaxed her hold but she glared at Theo. "Did you go out or not? I want the truth!"

"I didn't," said Theo. "I just made it up."

Rae leaned back in her seat. "What a weird kid you are. I can't figure you out."

Theo could tell she was still mad from their argument. Rae opened up a magazine and Theo pretended to read her book again. But her mind raced.

No, she hadn't been out on the deck. She hadn't met the Kaldors—they didn't exist. There was no John or Anna or Lisbeth or Ben—or Bingo or Beardsley—or Mum and Dad. They had all been a dream.

But *what* a dream! It had seemed utterly real. Theo went over every detail. She tried to freeze it all in her mind so she'd never forget. The house across the street from the cemetery, the mountain and the beach, the messy room she shared, the safety and the laughter and the love …

Sharon picked them up at the ferry terminal. "Theo!" she cried, wrapping her in a hug. "I haven't seen you since you were three! I'm so glad you're coming to live with me for a while."

Sharon was a large woman with an eager face. She wasn't pretty, like Rae. They didn't look like sisters. They didn't act like sisters, either.

"Hi," said Rae, pulling on her cigarette.

Sharon seemed afraid of her. "Good to see you again, Mary Rae," she mumbled. "I've been waiting for hours," she added timidly. "Didn't you say you were getting the one-o'clock ferry?"

Rae shrugged. "We missed it."

As they began the long drive into Victoria, Sharon asked her sister questions that Rae cut off briskly. Finally Sharon gave up and they drove in silence.

Theo felt so numb she barely noticed where they were going. Sharon parked the car in front of a modern brown and white apartment building called Crocus Court. Clipped bushes were spaced exactly the same width apart along the front.

"I hope you like it here, Theo," she said. "I was really lucky to get this apartment—it was built last year. This is the neighbourhood your mum and I grew up in—James Bay. It's so convenient, close to my office and the park and the beach."

She led Theo and Rae up the stairs to a small apartment. It had the same number of rooms as the one in Vancouver. But bright posters were pinned to its clean white walls and the furniture looked new.

"You can have my room, Theo," said Sharon. "I'll sleep on the sofa bed." She chuckled. "I spend most of my time there anyway—I'm a real couch potato!"

She turned on the television while she stirred spaghetti sauce in a tiny kitchen off the living-room. Theo sat on the couch beside Rae, glad of the TV's blare.

"You seem to be doing all right, Sharon," said Rae, as they ate around the kitchen table.

Sharon looked proud. "Thanks. I guess I am. I like my job and being a civil servant is really secure. I love being in my own place after having room-mates for so many years. We're really close to our old house, Mary Rae. Do you want to walk over there in the morning?"

"No, I want to get an early start. Where am I going to sleep?"

"You can have the sofa bed—I have a foamie I can use."

Soon after supper Theo said she was tired. She curled up in a soft bed covered in a frilly yellow bedspread. The

TV droned from the living-room, mixed with the occa-sional comment by Rae or Sharon.

Theo pulled the blanket right over her head. Then she escaped into her usual going-to-sleep fantasy—being in a proper family.

But now she *knew* the family. She could hear their voices: Ben's piping stories about Mortimer, Lisbeth's shrill demands, Anna's enthusing, John's careful expla-nations. She could feel the touch of Mum and Dad's hugs and kisses … of Bingo's slobbery tongue and Beardsley's rough one. She could smell John's underarms on the many days when he forgot to use the deodorant he had just begun to need. She could smell Beardley's litter box and Snow White's cage and Ben's socks and Mum's paints.

She could see them in glowing detail: Lisbeth's graceful body dancing a bumble-bee, the tufts of fly-away hair on Dad's balding head, Anna's braces stuck with bits of food, Ben's fingernails caked with dirt. Most of all she could see their eyes: Mum and John's dark and serious, Dad and Anna's a twinkling hazel, Ben's round and blue, and Lisbeth's like amethysts. All the eyes were gazing at Theo and all were brimming with love.

Theo let herself weep softly under the blanket. Then she tried to sleep. Maybe, just maybe, she could have the wonderful dream again.

But theo didn't dream at all. She opened her eyes to Sharon's yellow walls and was pierced with such a sharp grief she could hardly get out of bed. Now she had lost the Kaldors for good.

Sharon had taken the day off work. She tried again to persuade Rae to stay longer or at least to let her drive her to Swartz Bay, but Rae insisted on getting a bus to the ferry before breakfast. Theo stumbled into Sharon's car in a daze.

"Goodbye, Kitten," said Rae in front of the depot.

"Goodbye," muttered Theo.

"I'll come and visit," said Rae. "Maybe Cal can come, too." She looked more and more embarrassed. "Goodbye, then," she repeated, pulling hard on her cigarette.

Theo didn't see any point in saying it again. Rae reached forward to hug her; Theo went rigid, her arms pressed to her sides. Sharon hugged her sister, who stood just as stiffly. Finally they watched Rae pick up her backpack and join the crowd boarding the bus.

Sharon sighed. "Don't worry, Theo. I'm sure she'll come for a visit soon." When Theo didn't respond, she said brightly, "Shall we go back and have breakfast?"

"I don't care," said Theo.

13

Sharon made them pancakes. Theo ate mechanically, barely tasting the food. It was as if there were two Theos. Her real self was still in the Kaldor family; the person sitting at the table was like a puppet, lifting her fork to her mouth and nodding at Sharon's comments.

When they'd finished, Sharon invited her to sit beside her on the couch. She looked excited and scared. "Let's talk about our new life together. I'm not used to children, Theo. I helped look after you when you were little, but Ma did most of the work. I was out all day at my business course. What a cute little thing you were, with those big brown eyes! You were so good. Ma heard a woman on the radio say you could read to babies. She tried it and you actually listened! You never got restless or tore the pages. When you were a toddler, you'd sit on her lap for ages staring at the pictures."

Something in Theo stirred. "Did she ever read *Peter Rabbit*?" she asked.

"That was your favourite! Do you remember?"

"Sort of. When did my grandmother die?"

"When you were five. Two years after Rae took you back." Sharon sighed. "Ma never got over that. You cried and cried and you didn't understand why she couldn't come with you. At first Rae phoned once a month and we could talk to you. You always sounded bewildered, though. Rae came to Ma's funeral, but she left you in Vancouver with a friend. After that she stopped phoning. I would have come to see you, but I didn't know where you lived. The first time I heard from Rae was when she phoned last week. She had to try three S. Caffreys before she found me!" Sharon smiled. "You can imagine how excited I was to think of seeing you again!"

Sharon had one thing in common with Rae—she talked a lot. But she talked about *Theo*, not herself, so Theo had to try to pay attention.

It was strange to hear about things you didn't remember. All Theo had kept in her mind was hearing someone read to her in a kind voice. Now she knew it was her grandmother.

"Ma would be so glad you're back in Victoria," said Sharon. "Even if it's only for a little while. I'll try to take good care of you, Theo. It would be much easier if I didn't have to work every day, but that can't be helped. You'll have to start school tomorrow. It's not far—I can drive you there on the way downtown. I'm a secretary—I work in the Parliament Buildings. There's an after-school day care where you can go in the afternoons. I've drawn up a schedule so you'll know exactly what's happening every day."

Sharon picked up a paper on the table. It was titled "Theo's Schedule." Theo stared at it while her aunt went over each time slot.

7:30–8:30:   Get up, get dressed, breakfast, brush
               teeth, make bed.
8:30–8:40:   Drive to school.
9:00–12:00:   School.
12:00–1:00:   Lunch at school.
1:00–3:00:   School.
3:00–5:15:   Day care.
5:15–5:30:   Drive home.
5:30–6:00:   Help prepare supper.
6:00–6:30:   Supper.
6:30–8:00:   Help clear up supper, help make lunch
               for next day, do homework, watch TV,
               etc.
8:00:   Bath, brush teeth, go to bed.

The schedule was beautifully printed in neat lines; Sharon had obviously taken a lot of time over it. "The weekends will be more relaxed, of course," she said. "We'll shop for food on Saturdays. And on Sundays we'll go to church at the Cathedral. I often bowl on Sunday afternoons—you can come with me."

She smiled proudly. "It's not much different from the schedule I already follow—I like being organized. I wasn't sure what time nine-year-olds went to bed. Is eight too early? You can stay up later than that if you're not tired. Have you got any questions?"

The puppet Theo shook her head. "Eight is okay." She almost added she'd been walking to and from school and staying home alone since she was six, but she didn't want to hurt Sharon's feelings.

"Good. I'll post this on the refrigerator, so you can refer to it if you need to. Now, what would you like to do today? Shall I take you on a tour of Victoria?"

"I don't care," said Theo.

Her puppet self sat in the front seat of the car and tried to pay attention as Sharon pointed out the sights. She also talked a lot about her car. She'd saved up for it for years and explained technical things that Theo didn't understand.

It was a grey, misty day—winter again. Theo's eyes felt starved after weeks of feasting on the exuberant colours of spring.

After they'd driven slowly along Government Street and come back past Emily Carr's house, Sharon turned onto a busy street that skirted the sea. "This is Dallas Road," she said.

Theo gasped. Sharon looked over with surprise. "What's wrong?"

"I was just … sneezing," Theo said. She rubbed her eyes as the two Theos snapped together. Dallas Road! She'd *been* here!

She peered avidly out the window. This was the street she'd walked along so often on Sunday afternoons, the route she and Anna and Grace had taken on the way downtown.

Downtown … Theo suddenly realized that the places Sharon had just shown her—the chocolate shop and the old lamp-posts and the Empress Hotel and the Eaton Centre—were also where they had gone on that adventurous day.

She'd been here! She *knew* the waves lapping on the breakwater and the glimpse of the Olympic Mountains through the clouds.

If it had only been a dream, how could she dream about places she'd never seen?

Unless … "Have I been here before?" she asked Sharon. "I mean, when I lived here?" *Please* say no, she begged silently.

"Here? Along Dallas Road? Of course! You and Ma and I used to walk along here almost every Sunday." She took her eyes off the road for a second. "Do you remember, Theo? That's amazing!"

Theo split into two again. That was it. Part of her must

have remembered Victoria from when she was little and put it into her dream. She slumped back in her seat. Then it *had* been a dream.

But her heart pounded again when they passed another familiar landmark—the cemetery! She peered up the Kaldors' street to see if there was a tall old house at the top, but she couldn't see far enough.

"What about that cemetery?" she asked Sharon. "Did I ever go there?"

"Wow," said Sharon, "you *do* have a good memory! Yes, we often walked that far, to visit Dad's grave. He's buried there. He died when you were one. Ma's there with him now."

Disappointment flooded Theo again. Sharon drove as far as Uplands, then came back through Oak Bay. Theo barely glanced at the shoe store where Mum had taken her and the library where they'd gone every second Saturday. She must have been in those places when she was younger too. Recognizing parts of the city just made her more homesick for the Victoria in the dream.

THEY WENT BACK to the apartment for lunch. Then Sharon took out a piece of needlepoint and settled in front of a soap opera on the television.

"This is a boring program for children. Have you brought any toys or games or anything to play with?" she asked.

"A few," said Theo, "but I'm too old for them."

"Well, what would you like to do?" Sharon was looking longingly at the screen.

"I have a book," said Theo.

"Oh, good."

Theo went into her new room and looked in her bag. At the bottom were the few battered toys Rae had packed in Vancouver—and her doll. She'd forgotten all about Sabrina.

The old doll's rubber face smelled sour. Theo remembered Heather's clean new smell and put Sabrina back into the bag. She pulled out the library book instead.

It was a Mary Poppins story. Theo had loved the others but she couldn't get into this one. The happy Banks family wasn't *her* family. She put the book back in the bag too, and lay on her back trying to remember everything that had been in the room she'd shared with Anna and Lisbeth.

SHARON CALLED HER at four. They went for a walk to Theo's school, along pretty streets lined with small wooden houses. Down every street was a glimpse of the sea.

The school was only six blocks away. It was called St. Bridget's. "Your mother and I both went here," said Sharon. "When I registered you, I asked about my old teachers, but they've all retired. I loved this school. The nuns were so patient with us, and I always felt so secure."

"Did Rae like it?" asked Theo.

Sharon looked uncomfortable. "Mary Rae never liked any school. She was always getting into trouble and the kids were always talking about her. It was embarrassing to be her sister."

"What kind of trouble?"

"Oh, skipping classes and cheeking the teachers and smoking in the washrooms."

Theo almost smiled; that sounded like Rae.

"I'll show you our old house now," said Sharon. They walked a few blocks in the other direction until Sharon stopped in front of a blue cottage with forsythia blooming beside its front door.

"It looks much nicer now than when we rented it. It was brown then. A couple owns it—they've done a great job of renovating it." She gazed at the little house sadly. "What a lot happened here! You were born, and Dad and Ma both died. I remember the awful night Rae told them she was pregnant. She ..." But then she looked at Theo and blushed.

"What?" prompted Theo.

"Nothing," sighed Sharon. "There's no point wishing the past was different. It's all water under the bridge, as Ma used to say."

Theo stared at the house, trying to remember living here and playing in its tiny yard. It was all a blank. This house seemed much more like a dream than the Kaldors' house.

"SEVEN-THIRTY, time to get up!" called Sharon. Theo put on the red sweater and jeans Ms. Sunter had given her and sat down for breakfast.

Sharon looked worried. "I think you should wear a skirt, Theo. The other girls will be wearing tunics. You'll have a uniform too, but I can't get it until Saturday."

Theo went back to her room. The only skirt she could find was a thin cotton one stained with ketchup down one side. It was too long and its bright orange pattern clashed with the red sweater.

"Haven't you got anything nicer than that?" asked Sharon.

"This is my only skirt."

"Really? Mary Rae didn't dress you very well. Oh, I'm sorry, Theo, I didn't mean to criticize your mother. But why don't you have more clothes?"

"Because we were always broke," said Theo through a mouthful of cereal.

"Broke? But Mary Rae told me she had a good job!"

"She's a waitress. Before that she worked in a factory and a car wash. And sometimes we lived on welfare, especially when I was little."

"Welfare!" Sharon looked horrified. "But why didn't

she tell us? We could have helped her, or she could have come home and lived with us."

"I don't know why," said Theo.

"If only she'd gone back to school. You can't get much of a job when you only have grade ten. I thought she was doing all right, though. She said on the phone she'd send money for you every week!"

Sharon looked dismayed. Then she sighed and put on the resigned, everything-will-be-all-right look Theo was getting used to. "Well, there's nothing we can do about it. At least *I'm* not broke. I don't make much money, but I can afford to get you some decent clothes. I'll nip out to Eaton's at noon and pick you up a skirt you can wear for the rest of the week. And when we buy your uniform on Saturday we'll get you some other clothes too."

"Thank you," said Theo wearily. She was tired of adults fussing about her clothes.

SHARON TOOK THEO to the school office, kissed her goodbye, and left her. Theo once again followed a principal down the hall to a classroom. Counting the dream, this was the third time this year she'd started a new school.

She tried to armour herself with the warmth of the dream school to push out the chilly memories of the real ones. To her surprise, it worked. When the friendly kids smiled at her, she smiled back, pretending they were

Elise and Jasmin. When some of the girls gave sneering looks at the orange skirt, she pretended it was one of the new skirts Mum had bought for her. She met their eyes steadily until they turned away.

The teacher was a tired-looking woman called Mrs. Corelli. She smiled at Theo the way teachers always smiled at new kids and suggested she sit beside a girl called Skye.

Skye immediately began asking questions. When she found out where Theo lived, she clapped her hands. "That's only a few blocks away from my house!"

Skye told Theo she and her mother had moved to Victoria last fall. "We used to live up island, in the country near Duncan. I really miss it. We had a donkey and chickens and it was near a lake. But then my mum left my dad to live with Carol."

Skye's narrow face was dominated by thick glasses held together on one side with a Band-aid. "Will you be my best friend, Theo?" she asked at recess. "I had a best friend in Duncan, but I don't have one here yet."

Theo didn't answer. Skye was boring—all she talked about was her former home. She wasn't special, like Anna and Lisbeth. But when she pressed Theo for an answer, Theo shrugged and said, "I don't care." Skye's face filled with delight and she gave Theo her favourite eraser to keep.

The two of them ate their lunch together, but Theo had to go to after-school day care by herself. She walked to the classroom Mrs. Corelli had directed her to. "Day care" sounded like something for little kids.

An enthusiastic pair of young people greeted her—Meran and Jordan. They introduced Theo to a group of about fifteen children of various ages. The room was filled with books, magazines, games, paints and toys. There was even a television set. "You can do whatever you want," said Meran. "If the weather's nice we go outside and play soccer or something, but one of us is always inside, too."

Theo sank into a bean-bag chair in front of the TV. Another first day of school was over. It hadn't been that bad this time—just dull. Tears pricked her eyelids as she remembered her joyful first day at the dream school, where she'd had two sisters and a brother. But the puppet Theo, the one who was going through all the motions of living with Sharon, forced the tears back.

THAT EVENING in bed her real self won and let out her tears. She sobbed more and more loudly, hoping the TV noise would keep Sharon from hearing.

But then Sharon was at her side. "Theo! Oh, honey, don't cry! Do you miss your mother?"

She pulled Theo into her arms. "It's all right. I'll take

good care of you, and Mary Rae will come and visit soon, I'm sure."

Theo sank into Sharon's soft front and cried even more, pretending she was in Laura's—*Mum's*—arms instead.

14

Life with Sharon was predictable and safe. Each weekday clicked by in slots as neat as the ones on the schedule. On Saturday mornings the puppet Theo went to the supermarket with Sharon and helped carry in bags of food when they got back. On Saturday afternoons Sharon dropped her off at Skye's house, or sometimes she took both of them to a movie.

Sharon often went out with her best friend, Mandy, on Friday or Saturday night; then she got Tara, the teenaged girl down the hall, to look after Theo. Tara was sulky because she didn't have a boyfriend. "If I did, I wouldn't be stuck here babysitting," she complained. She slumped in front of the TV eating chips while Theo washed the dishes and put herself to bed.

Sharon took Theo to the Catholic cathedral every Sunday. Theo sat quietly, gazing at the green and gold and white ceiling and the jewel-like windows. A group with a flute and a guitar led the congregation in lively songs. "I Will Sing!" bellowed Sharon with the rest.

Theo wouldn't sing and she stayed in her pew when the priest invited all the children up to the altar. "I just want to watch," she said when Sharon tried to encourage her to take part. It was peaceful to sit passively and not have to do anything.

"Wait until you're used to it, then," was her aunt's comfortable reply.

Often Sharon took her bowling on Sunday afternoons. She let Theo try it, but she didn't like the heavy ball and the cracking sound it made when she dropped it too hard. She would sit with a soft drink and try to pay enough attention to cheer for Sharon's team when they won.

Sometimes she would lean against her aunt as they watched TV. Her body was soft and smelled of soap. Theo became as addicted to TV as Sharon. They talked about their favourite characters as if they were real people.

"I hope I'm not a bad influence on you," said Sharon. "Mary Rae told me that you read all the time, but I haven't seen you open up a book."

"I don't like reading any more," said Theo. It was true. Reading was dangerous; it made her yearn for things she couldn't have. The stories that unfolded on the screen were not real, like the ones in books; they didn't draw her in but were at a safe distance in their flickering world.

She didn't pretend any more, either; the puppet self that went through the motions of each day was too dull to make things up. She was simply *here*, doing what she was told in school, responding to other people when they talked to her. She noticed numbly that the kids in school accepted her and that Mrs. Corelli praised her for her work, but she didn't care. "You're a quiet one, aren't you?" Sharon told her. "Never mind. I was shy, too, when I was young. I make up for it now!"

Sharon told Theo how she longed to travel, to go to the places depicted in the posters on the walls. "I've never even been out of B.C., but Mandy and I are saving up to go to Europe." She bought lottery tickets every week, even though she'd never won anything.

Rae called twice. Theo held the phone a little away from her ear as her mother went on and on about Cal—the parties they'd been to, the trip they'd taken to Cultus Lake. She complained as usual about her boss and customers. She never said anything about coming to visit. At the end her voice became strained as she asked Theo how she was. "Good," said the puppet Theo.

Then Sharon talked to her for a few minutes. The second time, she asked Rae about sending money and Theo could hear her mother's angry excuses. After Rae hung up, Theo and Sharon paced the apartment separately for a few minutes. Then they gathered together on the couch, as if in mutual agreement to forget about Rae.

The puppet Theo didn't mind that her aunt treated her like a much younger child. Sharon even washed her hair and reminded her to brush her teeth every night. She never let Theo go anywhere alone—not even to Skye's house, or to school, or to play with Skye in Beacon Hill Park. "A little boy disappeared in Victoria a few years ago," she shuddered. "You can't be too careful."

She was like a nanny in an English book—but not a magic nanny like Mary Poppins. The puppet Theo tried not to think about magic; nothing would ever be magical again.

EVERY NIGHT, however, the real Theo dreamt about the Kaldors. Now she didn't want to dream about them, because these dreams weren't the same. They were like ordinary dreams—fragmented and patchy, sliding in and out of details; not like the long, marvellous dream she'd had on the ferry which had seemed so real and consistent. Her dreams still brought back the Kaldors, however—she could hear Lisbeth's giggle or Bingo's bark. They made her so unbearably homesick for the family, she tried to think of boring things before she went to sleep to keep the dreams away. It didn't work. Every night the real Theo woke up in tears that she was living with Sharon and not with the family she had once belonged to.

After a month with Sharon the real Theo began to come back in the daytime, too. The pleasant but dull sameness of her new life started to irk her. "This program is boring," she said one evening, as she and Sharon watched their usual Tuesday night sitcom.

Sharon looked surprised. "Do you think so? Go and do something else, then, if you're bored."

But there was nothing else to do. Theo strode around the small apartment and looked out the window. The trees across the street were a froth of pink blossoms and the ground beneath them blazed with crocuses. Spring was here—again!

Two boys bicycled towards the water. Theo remembered riding a bike with the family—puffing at the tops of hills, then coasting down with the wind in her face.

She turned around to Sharon. "Can I have a bike?"

"A bike?" Sharon looked apologetic. "Oh, hon, bikes are expensive."

"You could get me a secondhand one," said Theo. "Skye's mum got her one at the police sale."

"I'm sorry, Theo, but I'd worry too much about you if you had a bike. There's a lot of traffic around here and it gets much worse in the summer with all the tourists. What if you had an accident?"

"Could you borrow Skye's mum's bike and come with me?" Theo tried.

Sharon laughed. "Me on a bike? No, thanks—I'd rather drive. What's got into you tonight? Spring fever? Are you feeling okay?"

"Uh huh," muttered Theo. She went back to the window and Sharon went back to her program.

If only she could even go out for a walk! She couldn't help thinking of the walks the Kaldors took on Sundays along Dallas Road. The cemetery wasn't very far from here. She could walk there easily …

Seeing the cemetery would make her miss the family even more. But all at once Theo gave up trying not to think of them. Her puppet self went away for good. A surge of excitement filled the real Theo as she sat down beside Sharon again. She ignored the program and began to make a plan.

A FEW DAYS LATER Sharon got a terrible cold. Theo felt sorry for her as she lay on the couch on Saturday morning, surrounded by glasses of juice and wadded-up tissues. Sharon being sick, however, made Theo's plan much easier.

She lingered by the phone, waiting for it to ring. When it did, she snatched it up, listened for a few seconds, then said to Sharon, "It's Skye. She wants me to go to Goldstream Park for the day with her mum and Carol."

"That's nice," said Sharon, "especially when I'm so useless today. Let me talk to Robin." Sharon had become quite friendly with Robin and Carol.

Theo had expected this. "Is your mum there?" she asked into the receiver.

At the other end Skye giggled so hard that Theo was afraid Sharon would hear.

"They've gone to the store for a few minutes," she told Sharon.

"Let me talk to Skye, then."

Theo listened in agonized suspense. Could Skye stop laughing? Sharon said, "Uh huh … uh huh … and you'll be back at six? All right. Please thank your mother for including Theo."

She handed the phone back and blew her nose. "She says you'll be gone all day—you're going on a hike. That's good—you shouldn't be around me with all these germs. You'd better make yourself a sandwich and take one of those juice boxes. You'll have to walk to Skye's on your own, Theo. I can't move. Go straight there and phone me when you arrive."

"I'll be careful," said Theo, to make Sharon stop looking so worried. She made herself a peanut butter sandwich and put it with an apple and some juice and her anorak into the backpack Sharon had bought her. It was incredible that her guilt wasn't more apparent—it felt as if it were sprouting from her like prickles. She'd thought Sharon would insist on walking her to Skye's and she hadn't figured out how to stop her coming in to speak to Robin.

"Have a good time, hon," said Sharon. "No, don't kiss me—you might get my cold."

Theo blew her a kiss as she walked out the door.

SHE HEADED IN the direction of Skye's house in case Sharon was watching out the window. As she passed it a few streets over, she glanced at it gratefully and kept on going. Good for Skye. She'd thought the plan was fun when Theo had suggested it to her.

"But what are you going to do?" she'd asked.

Theo shrugged. "I just want to explore Victoria on my own."

"Good idea!" said Skye. "Maybe I could come with you!" She looked so eager that Theo almost said yes. She was relieved when Skye remembered that she and her mum had to visit someone on Saturday afternoon.

Theo turned towards Beacon Hill Park. Then she remembered she was supposed to phone Sharon. She looked for the quarter she'd put in her pocket and used a phone booth on the corner. "Have a good time," said her aunt again.

Theo felt so guilty that her legs quivered as she crossed Dallas Road. But as soon as she set out along the path beside the sea, she forgot about Sharon.

It was a bright March day. Early daffodils blew in the long grass beside the pond where kids and old men were sailing model boats. Below the cliffs the waves were wild, as if they were as excited as Theo. This was the first time she'd been alone since she'd arrived.

People smiled at her as they passed with their dogs and kids and bicycles. The cliff path was so familiar that

Theo felt as if John and Anna and Lisbeth and Ben were walking beside her. The Kaldors aren't real she reminded herself, but today she couldn't believe that they had only existed in her dream.

When she got near the cemetery, Theo's heart started pounding. She sat on a bench by the path and ate her apple, trying to calm down. Then she walked up the road until she reached one of the openings in the holly hedge.

The cemetery was exactly as it had been in the dream: a patchwork of rectangular mossy plots with towering trees above them. Theo even found the stone angel. This was where she'd spent some of her happiest times; but it was also where the wonderful dream had started to fade. She ate the rest of her lunch there, gazing up at the angel's serene face to give her courage. She knew where she was going next.

Standing up, she followed another walkway that led back to the upper part of the road. She kept her eyes down, afraid of the disappointment of not seeing the row of white houses across the street.

But when she finally looked up—they were there! Three neat houses almost alike, the highest one the house where she'd been so happy.

Theo's legs turned to rubber and she had to sit down on the grass. How could this be? It might make sense that she'd dreamt about streets and a path by the sea and a cemetery that she saw when she was little and somehow remembered. It might even make sense that she'd found the angel—maybe she saw that when she was little, too. Could she have once seen these houses as well?

Theo's body seemed to take over, making her stand up and walk on trembling legs across the road and up the sidewalk she knew so well. Her disbelieving eyes drank in the house near the top of the hill—its windows lined with orange and green, the design like a sunray where the roof peaked, the glimpse of the arbutus tree in the back. Her legs walked her up the same green steps and paused in front of the familiar brown door.

I *can't*! she cried inside. It was just a dream! But her shaking hand reached up and knocked on the door—first timidly, then louder.

The door opened slowly. A small boy stood there, holding a cookie. He was barefoot and his T-shirt had a dinosaur on it. Theo had seen that T-shirt many times.

"Ben?" she croaked. Then her voice and head cleared. "Ben, oh Benny," she cried. "It's me! I've come back!"

"Who are you?" asked the child.

THEO COLLAPSED into a puddle of arms and legs on the front doorstep. The next thing she knew she was being carried into the house by the same person who had once carried her in from the car after a late movie—Dad.

He laid her on the living-room couch while the others gathered around. Theo blinked as they came into focus:

Dad and Mum, John and Anna, Lisbeth and Ben. Bingo licked her face and whined. Beardsley hopped onto the arm of the couch and switched his tail while he watched her.

Mum wiped Theo's forehead with a cool wet cloth and kept asking if she were all right. But she didn't call her Theo. The family gazed at her with curiosity—as if they were looking at a stranger.

"What's your name?" Mum asked, as Theo sat up and Anna handed her a glass of water.

"It's me—Theo!"

Six puzzled faces stared at her. "Theo who?" Dad asked gently.

Theo felt like crying—they didn't remember her! This was as bad as when she had started to fade. No, worse—they could see her, but they didn't know her! "Caffrey," she whispered.

"Where do you live? Why did you come to our door?" demanded Lisbeth.

Theo winced at her blunt words. If she really was a stranger to them she'd better be careful. She thought fast. "I—I live with my aunt in James Bay. I was walking up the street and I—I felt dizzy, so I stopped at your house for help."

"But why are you on your own?" asked Dad. "Does your aunt know where you are?"

Theo was too stunned to lie. She shook her head.

"I went for a walk by myself, but she thinks I'm at my friend's. She's going to be really upset with me."

The children looked sympathetic and Bingo licked her face.

"I think she'll just be relieved to know you're all right," said Mum. "What's your phone number, Theo? I'll phone your aunt and tell her we'll bring you home. On the way we'll take you to the clinic up the street and have them check to see that you're really all right."

Theo whispered her number to Mum then sank back against the cushions. Dad introduced everyone and she tried to pretend this was the first time she'd heard their names. "And I'm Dan and my wife is Laura," he finished. Theo tried not to think of them as Dad and Mum.

Laura came back into the living-room. "Your Aunt Sharon is shocked of course, but she's not angry at you, Theo. Let's get you into the car—can you walk?"

Theo struggled to her feet and let them help her into the car. They all wanted to come, but only Laura and Anna took her to the clinic. A doctor prodded her and took her pulse. "You're fine," she said. "Just take it easy for the rest of the day. Sometimes people faint for no reason. If it happens again, though, be sure to go to your own doctor, all right?"

"All right," whispered Theo.

Anna was as friendly as she had been when Theo had first met her on the ferry. "How long have you lived in

Victoria? What school do you go to?" she asked on the way to Sharon's.

Theo answered in spurts, still shocked that Anna didn't know her.

They both walked her into the apartment. "Oh, Theo!" cried Sharon, forgetting her cold and kissing her many times. "*Thank* you," she told Laura fervently. "I don't know what made her do such a thing. She's usually so well behaved!"

Laura smiled. "You can't always predict *what* they'll do. Believe me, I know—I have four!"

"Won't you stay and have coffee?" asked Sharon. She'd got dressed and tidied away all the tissues and glasses.

She and Laura sat on the couch while Laura told Sharon what the doctor had said. Theo and Anna sat on the rug nibbling cookies.

Theo couldn't speak, but Anna whispered, "Aren't grown-ups boring? I think it was really brave of you to go somewhere on your own. Once my older brother and I sneaked out at night and played in the cemetery! It was really spooky. We got back without being caught and no one ever found out!"

She tossed back her shining cap of hair and gave the same rich laugh she had always had. A thrill went through Theo. It was awful that Anna didn't remember her, but she was *Anna*—she really existed!

"What are you two muttering about?" smiled Laura. "I

think we'd better go, Anna. I hope you'll be all right, now, Theo. It was nice to meet you, Sharon." She shook hands with both of them and they left, Anna winking at Theo over her shoulder.

Theo almost ran after them. "Don't go!" she wanted to call. "I've just found you again!" She stood in the doorway until Sharon's voice made her turn around.

Sharon was quivering. Theo braced herself; would her aunt hit her?

But instead of being angry Sharon broke into sobs. "Oh, Theo honey, what a bad scare you gave me! I couldn't stand it if anything happened to you!" Her face was red and swollen with tears and her cold. "How could you lie to me like that? I thought we were friends!"

It was hard to focus on Sharon when Theo's whole being was concentrated on the Kaldors. But her aunt looked so baffled and hurt, she took her hand. "I'm sorry. I just wanted to go for a walk on my own and I thought you wouldn't let me."

"Of course I wouldn't let you! Look what happened!"

"I'll never do it again," said Theo. "I promise. And I'll never lie again, either."

"I hope not." Sharon stiffened. "Mary Rae was always lying to our parents. I hope you're not going to take after her."

"I'm not! I'm *nothing* like her!"

"Of course you aren't, hon. You're just yourself." Sharon

blew her nose and smiled weakly. "You're an odd kid, though. Mary Rae warned me about that. Why would you want to go for a walk all by yourself?"

When Theo didn't answer, Sharon hugged her. "I think we both need to lie down. On Monday I'm taking you to my doctor for a complete physical. We won't talk about this again, Theo. I hope you've realized what can happen when you do something so foolish."

Theo escaped to her bed. She lay on her back, staring at the sun that turned the drawn blind a glowing yellow. Her mind danced with all that happened and she kicked up her feet with excitement.

Her time living with the Kaldors *hadn't* been a dream! They really existed!

That meant it must have been magic after all. Somehow her new-moon wish had come true. She had spent all that happy time with the family in the sort of magic adventure that happened in books. Then, for some reason, the magic had ended and she'd been back on the ferry again at the same moment she'd left.

It was just like a story; rather like time-travel stories she'd read, except she'd gone sideways in time, not backwards. Stories were more complete, however, and they gave reasons for the magic.

Theo didn't care. She hugged herself. It had happened after all—she had once belonged to the Kaldors, in some kind of strange fantasy that had ended with no explanation. But now she'd found them again.

The trouble was, they didn't remember her. Were the children just pretending not to know her in front of their parents? Was it part of the magic that only *Theo* could remember?

She pondered her family in greedy detail. Lisbeth had lost a tooth and Anna had had her hair cut. John was taller. She had been with them such a short while, she hadn't had time to notice other things or to talk to them, except to Anna.

Somehow she had to see them again. Then she would *make* them remember and everything would be as perfect as it had been before.

15

The next morning Theo received a phone call.

"Theo?" said an eager voice. "This is Anna Kaldor, the person you met yesterday? How are you feeling?"

Theo's voice shook. "Fine."

"We were wondering if you'd like to come over this afternoon."

"Oh! I—I *would*! Just a minute, I'll ask my aunt."

After Sharon, too, asked Theo how she was feeling, she said it was okay. Theo listened to Anna telling her what time to come. She could barely squeak a goodbye.

"It's nice of them to ask," said Sharon. "Are you sure you want to?"

"Yes, yes, *yes*!" cried Theo, dancing around the kitchen.

Sharon looked surprised. "You're usually so shy! And you've only just met them. But Anna looked like a nice girl and I liked Laura—she seems so serene, somehow. Did you say she was an artist?"

"She's a graphic artist," said Theo. "She paints wonderful cards of dressed-up animals and kids playing."

"Did she show them to you?"

"Uh huh." Theo flushed. Was that a lie? Laura *had* shown them to her—but not yesterday. She went to get ready for church before Sharon could ask her more.

"What a great old house," said Sharon as they walked up the Kaldors' steps after lunch. Theo stood silently in the hall as Sharon met the rest of the family. She barely heard her aunt's goodbye as she drank them in. She was home.

"We're glad you could come, Theo," said Laura. "The girls begged to see you again. I hope you're feeling better now."

Theo knew she couldn't call her "Mum"—not yet, not until she'd figured out how to make them remember her. But she gave Laura a huge smile. "I feel *great*," she assured her.

But right away, things began to go wrong. "Come and see our room," said Lisbeth. She pulled Theo up the stairs, Anna following.

Theo trembled as she stared at the familiar, messy space. But her bed and dresser weren't there. She opened her mouth to remind them that she'd once slept here. But she couldn't get out the words, as Anna and Lisbeth competed to show her things.

"This is Heather, my best doll." Lisbeth put the red-haired doll in Theo's arms and Theo hugged the familiar shape for comfort.

"That's my favourite hockey player," said Anna, pointing to the poster by her bed.

"I *know*," Theo began, "I—"

"—Oh, do you like him, too?" asked Anna.

"This is my eraser collection," said Lisbeth. She pulled down a box from the top of the bookshelf and knocked off a china horse.

"Lisbeth!" Anna picked up the horse. Its leg was missing. "Look what you've done, you stupid klutz! You're an idiot!" She punched Lisbeth's shoulder.

Lisbeth started a high-pitched, whining wail. "Owww! You hurt me! You're not supposed to hit me, Anna! And Daddy said you're not supposed to call me an idiot!"

"Then you're a—a person of low intelligence! You broke my favourite horse! I'm telling!" Anna ran out of the room.

Theo stood there in bewilderment while Lisbeth continued to cry. The two of them had never hit each other or spoken to each other so meanly … *before.*

Laura came into the room, followed by Anna. "Stop that awful noise, Lisbeth! Tell me how Anna's horse got broken."

"It was an *accident*," cried Lisbeth. "It fell off the shelf!"

176

"She's a dingle-brain!" fumed Anna.

"I am not!" Lisbeth shoved her sister.

"That's enough!" Laura's voice was stern. "I don't want to hear another word! How can you be so rude when you have a guest? If you don't stop arguing this minute, Theo will have to go home. Do you understand?"

They both sniffed and nodded.

"That's better. I'm sure I can mend the horse. Help me find the leg." They all got down on the floor and Laura found it under the bookshelf.

Anna looked embarrassed after Laura took the horse downstairs to glue it. "Sorry, Theo. It's just that Lisbeth's such an—"

"If you say that word I'll *scream*. Then Mum will come up again," warned Lisbeth.

Theo watched each of them pull back her anger. Before, they had seemed so close. Didn't they like each other any more?

"Theo, come and see *my* room," called Ben from the hall. Theo was glad to get away from the feud. She followed him into his familiar, smelly room. "Where's your iguana?" she asked him fondly.

Ben looked puzzled. "What's a gwana?"

"You know—you used to have an iguana called Mortimer. You fed him flies and bees and kept him in a cage. Sometimes you and I took him for a walk in the cemetery, remember?"

Ben stared. "You're *silly*!" He ran into the girls' room. "Theo's silly! She's making things up about me!"

"Don't be rude, Ben," said Anna crossly. "Theo can say anything she likes. You're the one who's silly. You're always pretending things, so why can't she?"

"I'm *not* silly!" shouted Ben. "I don't like you and I don't like Theo!" He ran out, slamming their door.

Theo's eyelids pricked. How could he say that? Sweet Ben, whom she'd spent so many happy times with before …

"Do you want to go outside, Theo?" asked Anna. Lisbeth followed them, but she was sulking so much she'd stopped speaking.

The three of them climbed up the mountain, ran along the beach and explored the cemetery. Every time Anna told her about something, Theo wanted to say she had been here before. But the longer she put it off, the harder it was to begin.

Lisbeth was so silent Theo wondered if she was mad at her as well. But when they finally rested on the grass underneath the angel, Lisbeth asked Theo a question. "Why do you live with your aunt instead of your parents?"

"Don't pry, Lisbeth," said Anna, but she looked curious, too.

They had never asked her questions before. Theo took a deep breath; she may as well tell them. "I used to live in Vancouver with my mother," she began, "but she lives with her boyfriend now and he doesn't want me, so I came over here to live with my aunt."

"That must have been really hard," said Anna.

"Are you going to stay living here?" Lisbeth asked.

"I don't know," said Theo. "Nobody says."

There was an awkward silence. Theo squirmed at the girls' pity. She could tell they thought she was strange.

Before, she had never felt this uncomfortable. Then they had just accepted her, with no questions about her past. Then she had been their sister. That was getting harder and harder to believe.

Finally Lisbeth spoke. "*I've* been to Vancouver—lots and lots of times. We go on the ferry to visit Grannie and Gramps. They live on the North Shore. It's really pretty there. Was it pretty where you lived, Theo?"

Theo shook her head. "No. It was all grey. Not like here."

She was thinking of what Lisbeth had just said. "Do you like going on the ferry?" she asked carefully.

"Oh, yes!" said Lisbeth. "We run up and down the deck and pretend to fly in the wind."

"I like the way all the kids play at the front of the lounge," said Anna. "We always meet new people there."

Theo shivered inside. "Did you—did you go on the ferry in February?" Her voice was so low she had to repeat her question.

"February? No, we haven't been to Vancouver since Christmas, but we're going for Easter," said Anna.

"Oh." It was too much to hope for. She *knew* they'd been on the ferry; she knew how they pretended to fly and played in the lounge. But they didn't remember.

And there was no point in telling them, because they weren't the same. They acted as if they had just met her yesterday. They already thought she was strange; they would think she was even stranger if she told them she'd once lived with them. They'd never believe her.

Had she lived with them? Of course she had! How else could she know them so well? But that magic time seemed more and more distant as the afternoon went on.

BEFORE DINNER Theo sat in the den with the others and watched TV. Ben still gave her insulted glances. Anna and Lisbeth still muttered to each other when their parents were out of the room.

"John!" Dan came to the door. "Why haven't you taken out the garbage?"

"I forgot," mumbled John.

"This is the third time you've forgotten this week! I'm tired of reminding you. There'll be no allowance for you this Saturday."

"No allowance!" cried John. "But I wanted to get some new tapes!"

"That's too bad," said Dan. "Maybe this will teach you

to remember. Now get going on that garbage!" Theo had never heard his voice sound so harsh.

John stomped out of the room. He hadn't spoken to Theo since his curt hello—as if she were only a friend of his sisters. She couldn't believe he was the same John who had taught her so patiently how to ride a bike.

Only Bingo and Beardsley treated her the same. Beardsley rubbed against her legs, his throat rumbling, and Bingo followed Theo around all afternoon, as if he were overjoyed that she was back.

"Bingo sure seems to like you," said Lisbeth.

"Just push him away if he's a nuisance," said Anna.

"It's okay." Theo buried her head in Bingo's soft neck and sniffed up his yeasty smell. She was beginning to long for the day to end, so she could go back to Sharon's and cry.

AT DINNER all the Kaldors' bad moods came together in one noisy complaint.

"I don't want to sit beside Theo!" said Ben.

"Behave yourself, Ben—what will Theo think of you?" Laura made him stay in his place, but he kicked at Theo's foot all through the meal.

"Someone has been at my books again," said Dan. "I found two lying on the floor in the den. I've told you again and again to put them back when you've finished with them."

John glowered at his father. "Don't look at *me*."

"It was probably Lisbeth," said Anna.

"It wasn't!" squealed Lisbeth. "I can't even read those thick books!"

"Okay, simmer down," said Dan. "But it's got to be someone in this family who keeps leaving them around—who else could it be?"

"Dan, for heaven's sake stop fussing!" said Laura. "It's probably you who left them there—you've just forgotten."

"It's *not* me!" Dan's voice sounded just as aggrieved as Lisbeth's. "All I ask is—"

"Dad, *please* change your mind about my allowance."

"Mummy, Anna won't pass me the pickles and I've asked her three times!"

"I don't like this fish. Pirates don't *eat* fish."

"Shush!" Laura raised her hand. "*Everyone* shush!" She looked around at the sulky family and sighed. "I'm sorry, Theo, I don't know what you must think of us. You've come on a bad day. We're not always like this."

You were *never* like this before, thought Theo miserably.

"Will you come again?" asked Anna, after Sharon arrived. "Can you come on Saturday for the whole day?"

Sharon turned around from admiring one of Laura's paintings in the hall. "She'd love to, wouldn't you, Theo?" Theo couldn't answer.

"They're so nice!" said Sharon on the way home.

"Their house has such pretty things in it and Dan and Laura are so interesting. I think the kids will be good friends for you. I hope you don't mind that I said you wanted to go back."

Theo wondered if she minded. The Kaldors had been such a disappointment. Yet something in her still couldn't resist them. At least, when she was there, she could re-live the other time.

"What's the matter?" The light was red and Sharon turned to look at Theo. "You seem so sad. Didn't you have a good time?"

Theo tried to sound more cheerful. "I'm okay. Just tired."

"It's a good thing you're having that check-up tomorrow," said Sharon. "But I'm not surprised you're tired. You're not used to a large lively family, after boring me! You don't have to be friends with them. But why not give them one more try?"

"I don't care," shrugged Theo.

16

Theo stood in the hall and clenched her fists as Anna and Lisbeth clattered down the stairs to greet her. All week the real Kaldors and the magic Kaldors had clashed in her mind. Maybe on this visit the family would be the perfect one she had known.

At least they were in better moods today. Anna only called Lisbeth an idiot once and John even asked Theo how she was. Ben had forgotten his anger; he showed Theo his new plastic dinosaurs. Anna's face was tender as she braided Lisbeth's hair and Dan hugged John after he played his new piece for them. To Theo's relief their best selves—the only selves Theo had known before—still existed.

There was even a moment before lunch that came close to the bliss she had once experienced here. Dan had made pizza dough and everyone was creating his or her own pizza from the ingredients he'd arranged on the kitchen table. Arms got tangled as they reached for green peppers and cheese and onions. As John helped Ben cut a piece of salami into a smile, Lisbeth and Laura began singing "Aiken Drum."

"'And his mouth was made of pizza, pizza, pizza,'" they all yelled. Theo joined in and they smiled at her. She had sung this with them before, in the car on the way back from skiing. While the song lasted, she was back—back in that time when she'd really belonged.

But as the day went on, Theo began to realize she could never really belong. The magic was over—only the real Kaldors remained. In the real family that moment of perfect harmony in the kitchen rarely came. Someone was always out of kilter and complaining or arguing or moody.

And now Theo was an outsider. John and Anna didn't protect her, Lisbeth and Ben didn't adore her, and Laura and Dad didn't hug or kiss her. Often someone referred to a person or an incident Theo didn't know about.

And now they asked her questions—uncomfortable questions.

"What does your mother do?" Anna wanted to know, as she and Theo and Lisbeth sat on top of the mountain after lunch.

"She's a waitress."

"Where's your dad?" asked Lisbeth.

Theo squirmed. "I don't know. He lives in Greece, but I've never met him."

"Never met him!" Lisbeth looked shocked. "Poor Theo!"

"That's not unusual, Lis," said Anna. "Theo's parents probably got divorced when she was a baby, like Ashley Forster's. He must have met you when you were younger, Theo—you just don't remember. Maybe you can visit him one day. That would be wonderful, going to Greece!"

A wave of resentment went through Theo. Anna thought everything had simple solutions. Theo's life was so complicated compared to theirs.

Suddenly she wanted to shock them. "I don't even know my father's last name," she told them. "I'll *never* meet him."

"But doesn't he send money to your mother?" asked Anna. "Ashley's father does, even though he lives in Australia."

"He doesn't even know I exist. We've never had *any* money. My mother had crumby jobs or we lived on welfare."

"Welfare!" they cried.

"Sometimes we had to panhandle, too," said Theo. "I danced and people gave us money."

Anna looked horrified. "But that's begging!"

"We didn't have a choice," said Theo. She watched a ship glide by on the horizon. Then she took a deep breath and told them everything. How hungry she'd been sometimes, how often they'd moved, what it was like to be alone most of the time in cold apartments full of cockroaches and mice. They would probably despise her, but she couldn't help it—she felt full of power as she made the details of her life in Vancouver come alive for them.

"It's like a *story*," said Lisbeth. "Like the little match girl story Daddy read to us."

Anna's clear eyes brimmed with tears. "I can't believe people really live like that."

"Lots of people do," said Theo.

"I think you're really brave," said Lisbeth.

"So do I," said Anna.

To Theo's surprise they were gazing at her not with pity or scorn, but with respect.

"Thanks for telling us that," said Anna quietly. "Let's go back now." Lisbeth took Theo's hand and kept hold of it all the way down.

Anna's friend Grace Leung came over for a while and Theo had to pretend she'd never met her. When they started talking about school she risked a careful question. "Who teaches grade four at your school?"

"Mrs. Hutchinson," said Anna.

"Not Ms. Tremblay?"

"There's no one at our school called that," said Grace. "Why do you want to know?" She looked wary, as if she thought Theo was weird.

"Oh, no reason. I once knew a teacher called Ms.

Tremblay and I—I heard she moved to Victoria," said Theo lamely.

Grace still looked suspicious, but Anna gave Theo a reassuring smile. "Maybe she's at a different school," she said. "Do you guys want to try our new computer game?"

Theo followed them downstairs, dizzy with confusion. Some details of her former time here were the same as before—like Grace. But Ms. Tremblay didn't exist! Maybe the kids in Ms. Tremblay's class didn't exist either. It was all so confusing she tried to just lap up the soothing warmth that Anna and Lisbeth were showing her.

THEO WAS EXHAUSTED by the end of the day. The Kaldors seemed to expect her to ask *them* questions, too—to participate, to make an effort to know them as if they'd never known each other before. It was hard work, becoming an involved new friend instead of a passively accepted member of the family.

By the end of the day she felt glimmerings of a new kind of belonging—as if they had each put out fragile filaments that knotted them together.

"We're going skiing on Monday for Spring Break," said Anna, "but come and see us again when we get back, okay?"

"Are you going to Mt. Washington?" asked Theo.

"Yes—how did you know?"

"I just guessed," said Theo.

"It's a great place!" said John. He went on to tell Theo about his favourite runs. Theo listened longingly, remembering her exhilarating attempts at skiing when she'd gone with them. If only she could go again!

"How did you like the Kaldors this time?" Sharon asked her on the way home.

"They were … all right," said Theo slowly. They would never be the same as before—she knew that now. But the present family was better than no family at all.

SHARON ARRANGED for Theo to spend the first four days of Spring Break with Skye. "I wish I could get the whole week off," she sighed. "They won't let me take my holidays until the summer."

"Who are these people you've been visiting?" demanded Skye. She sounded jealous.

"Just some friends."

"Did you know them before you moved here?"

Theo started to say yes, then she shook her head.

"Then you knew me first!" said Skye. "I don't think it's fair that you spend all your time with them."

"I've only been there twice," said Theo.

Skye still looked hurt and Theo realized how much she'd ignored her since she'd found the Kaldors again. She never went to Skye's after school and even in class she barely spoke to her.

But Skye was so needy and dull. She only wanted to

be with Theo so she could talk about her father and her old home.

Robin, Skye's mother, was a nurse. Her companion, Carol, was a freelance writer who worked at home. They were both funny, nice women; Theo didn't understand why Skye always seemed so dissatisfied. All she and Skye ever did was play with Barbies, like much younger kids ... like Lisbeth!

Anna and Lisbeth weren't as perfect as they'd been before, but they were still much more special than Skye. Theo thought of them constantly as she and Skye watched TV, dressed the Barbies in their endless outfits, or went on outings to the museum and the beach and movies with Carol. She was relieved to get away from Skye when Sharon took her to Nanaimo for three days.

By THE NEXT SATURDAY Theo was bursting to see the Kaldors again. Anna had told her that it was her eleventh birthday; Theo was to come early and help get ready for her party.

Theo had spent a long time picking out a mystery novel for Anna in the store Sharon had taken her to in Nanaimo. "Don't you want some books for yourself?" she had asked.

"No, thanks," said Theo. She still didn't feel like reading. Her life was getting so interesting again, she didn't need stories. She grinned to herself as she wrapped the book.

Anna didn't know that Theo knew all her favourite authors.

Once again, it was hard work being with the family. But Theo was getting used to it. She asked lots of questions about skiing, she praised Lisbeth's new sweater and she listened patiently to Ben's description of a bear that only he had seen.

She also answered their questions in careful detail, relating what she'd done in Nanaimo as if she were telling a story. "Sharon's friends took us to a place where there were goats on the roof!" she said, enjoying the way Lisbeth's eyes lit up.

Six girls arrived for Anna's party. Theo tried not to think of her other party, when she'd received a new bike and Dan and Laura had served a special dinner. Today they were going to a movie after cake and ice cream.

Anna raved about her book. "How did you know I like this series?"

"I just guessed," said Theo.

Lisbeth leaned against Theo as Anna opened the rest of her presents. "Sometimes I feel as if we've known you for a long long time," she whispered.

You have, thought Theo sadly. She could never tell them that now.

THEO AND SHARON spent a lot of time talking about the Kaldors. Sharon always wanted to know exactly what they'd done. Her face was envious as Theo described Anna's party. "I always wanted to have lots of brothers and sisters," she said. "They sound like a perfect family."

"I used to think they were," said Theo. "I mean, the first time I visited them," she added. Was that a lie? It wasn't the first time Sharon thought she meant, but it was true.

Sharon seemed to be waiting for Theo to explain. "I still really like them," said Theo. "But sometimes they argue and sometimes I feel left out."

Sharon smiled. "Oh, well, hon … *all* families argue. You should have heard ours! I'm sure they get along better than we did. We were all so different. Dad was so set in his ways and Mary Rae was so rebellious. She could never please him, so Ma spoiled her to make up for it. And they always took it for granted that I wouldn't be any trouble." She sighed. "But I shouldn't burden you with my memories. You know, Mandy's family is sort of like the Kaldors. Even though they're all grown up and the kids have left home, when I go over there for Christmas or birthdays it's as if they belong to a special club. They're so close-knit—and they can't help shutting me out." She hugged Theo. "Never mind, we have each other, right?"

Theo wriggled inside the hug. She *liked* Sharon—but it wasn't the same.

A secret club … that was exactly it. She had been to Mandy's family's house with Sharon for a few Sunday dinners. They were like the Kaldors—like a friendly club to which one could never really belong. Her experience was worse than Sharon's, however, because once she had belonged.

"Why don't you ask Anna and Lisbeth here one Saturday?" suggested Sharon. "It doesn't seem right that you always go there."

"No, thank you," said Theo hastily. She went into her room to escape from Sharon's hurt look. How could she explain that she had to be in their house? Then she could sometimes pretend that she still lived there.

17

Theo spent the next Saturday with the Kaldors as well. They lent her a bicycle—the same one she'd ridden before.

"It's too bad you haven't got your bike from Vancouver," said Anna.

"I didn't have a bike. I've never had one," said Theo.

"How did you learn how to ride one, then?" asked Lisbeth, as Theo passed her on the road.

"I just know," called back Theo. Because John taught me! she wanted to add. She pedalled hard, then coasted, a grin on her face. Knowing how to ride a bike proved absolutely she'd once lived with the family.

The weekend before Easter Theo was asked to the Kaldors for a sleepover. "That would work out really well for me," said Sharon. "Mandy and Lynn want me to go to Saltspring Island with them."

Theo was ecstatic about sleeping and waking up in the house again. She wondered where they'd put her.

"You're sleeping in our room," Lisbeth told her. She showed Theo a narrow rollaway cot, placed against the same wall where Theo used to sleep. Theo could hardly wait to get into it.

Finally it was time to go to bed. First Dan read them a chapter from *Swallows and Amazons*. Theo had forgotten how much she'd once loved this story; how powerfully books could pull you in so that you forgot where you were.

The three girls talked and giggled for a long time in the dark. Finally Lisbeth said crossly, "Shut up, you guys! I want to go to sleep!" She was instantly quiet. Anna murmured a few more comments to Theo then she, too, became silent.

Theo tossed for hours. Even after Laura and Dan came up to bed, she was still awake. She lay on her back and stared up at the skylight where she'd heard the rain dripping on her first day. If only she could sleep, maybe she'd wake up and find herself a part of the family again.

But she wouldn't. That had been magic, but this was real. A very pleasant real. She was spending a whole weekend with her best friends. But the magic had spoilt her. She was greedy for more, to belong again.

Now she didn't belong anywhere. Life with Sharon was okay, but Theo knew she couldn't stay there forever. One day she'd have to go back to Rae—a prospect she usually kept pushed deep in her mind. But tonight Theo kept thinking of her mother. Did Rae miss her? She hadn't phoned for weeks. Was she happy living with Cal? Would *Theo* have to live with Cal? She shuddered at the thought of seeing him every day.

Theo threw back her hot quilt. She smoothed Heather's hair—Lisbeth had let her sleep with her. They had forgotten to pull down the blinds; through the other window she could see a crescent moon.

A *new* moon … Theo got up and crept to the window. All the treetops in the cemetery danced in the wind; the moon was a radiant bow above them.

She could try wishing on the moon again! "I wish I *really* belonged to this family," whispered Theo. It had worked before—why not now?

Theo sat on the chest by the window, staring out at the cemetery. She wasn't asleep, yet she wasn't really awake; she was in a kind of trance, the way she used to be in school in Vancouver.

A movement outside made her glance to the left. A figure was coming out of the entrance to the cemetery: a woman. She walked across the street in a smooth, gliding movement. It was hard to make out her features in the dark, but she was tall and angular, wearing a shapeless coat.

She came closer and Theo could see her better by the streetlight. The woman's face looked strangely familiar. Plain and gaunt, with wispy hair. She looked distracted.

The woman came up the steps and Theo lost sight of her. She must be planning to visit Laura and Dan, but why so late? There was no knock; maybe the woman had decided it was too late, also. Theo waited for her to come back down the steps and walk away, but no one appeared.

She was so tired now; maybe she was dreaming. She got back into bed and sank into sleep. Later she began shivering, vaguely aware that her quilt had slipped to the floor. She was too soundly asleep to wake up and get it.

Then warmth enveloped her as the quilt was tucked around her. Theo smiled and snuggled deeper into her dreams.

FOR THE FIRST FEW MINUTES of the morning she couldn't tell if her wish had come true. Anna threw her pillow at her exactly the way she used to and Lisbeth jumped on her bed. Theo was flooded with hope; was she really back?

But then Lisbeth said, "I hope we have time to finish our puzzle before Sharon comes to get you."

Theo's spirits sank. The wish hadn't worked; she was still just a friend, not a sister. She turned her head to hide her swelling tears.

"What's the matter, Theo?" asked Anna.

"Nothing," said Theo, holding up her head so the tears wouldn't drip. She wiped her eyes on her nightgown as she pulled it off.

She felt better at breakfast. Dan made waffles and Theo wolfed down their comforting sweetness as fast as the others. Squished between Ben and Lisbeth, she pretended that she was part of this noisy circle every morning.

"Did you have a good sleep, Theo?" asked Laura.

"Not at first," said Theo. "I got up and sat by the window." Then she remembered what she'd seen. "I thought I saw someone come to the door," she said. "A woman."

"That's odd. Did she knock?" asked Dan.

"No—she sort of disappeared. I was too tired to see her properly."

"You were probably dreaming," said Laura.

"Maybe you didn't even get up," said Anna. "Sometimes I dream I get up when I don't."

"Sometimes I dream I have to pee and in my dream I get up and go to the bathroom—but I don't!" said Ben.

"And then you wet the bed," said Lisbeth. "Only babies do that."

Theo didn't listen to them argue. She thought of the strange woman and how familiar she'd looked. Then she remembered how she'd lost her quilt during the night but had been covered up in the morning. But she could have done that in her sleep, too. Maybe Anna was right and she'd dreamt she'd got up. Maybe even her wish had only been a dream.

It was a blustery, rainy day. In the morning they stood under umbrellas and watched Anna and Grace's soccer team lose their game.

After lunch Dan made a fire and they sat in the living-room. Dan read a magazine, Ben played with his Lego and John joined the girls as they continued to put together the huge jigsaw puzzle they'd started yesterday.

Laura looked up from a letter she was writing. "Isn't this nice, being in here all together like this!"

"But—but don't you usually sit in here?" asked Theo. They hadn't since she'd started visiting, she realized.

Laura laughed. "We're too busy—someone is always being picked up or driven somewhere."

Theo sighed. *Before* they had sat in here every evening—all of them, as peacefully as they were right now. The fire crackled, Bingo groaned in his sleep, and she tried to forget she had to go back to Sharon's in a few hours.

She lost interest in the puzzle and went over to the chair by the bookshelf. One of the books was lying face up on the floor. Theo picked it up. It was old and grimy, with a faded cover showing two children standing around a sundial. It didn't look very interesting, but she remembered how the ugliest books in school libraries were often the best ones. It was such a long time since she'd read a book; maybe she should try this one.

"What have you got there, Theo?" asked Laura.

"*In Summer Time* by Cecily Stone. I found it on the floor."

"That's the lady who used to live here!" said Anna.

"Now, how on earth did that book get down here?" said Dan. "It's supposed to be shelved upstairs with the other Victoria writers! I wish this family would put books back when you've done with them."

"It wasn't me," said Lisbeth. "That book's too hard for *me* to read."

"What does it matter, Dan?" said Laura calmly. She smiled at him. "You're obsessed. Books are meant to be read, not kept in neat order. Cecily Stone was a children's writer," she explained to Theo. "She lived in this house for years."

"She was born here," said Dan. "She wrote two books, then she died of cancer. Her books were excellent, but they're out of print now. I have several copies of each title—I keep a lookout for them in secondhand stores."

"I've read them both," John told Theo. "The first one's historical and that one's a time travel."

"They're really good," said Anna. "I read them, too."

"When did she live here?" asked Theo.

"Let's see…," said Dan. "She died in 1956—so about forty years ago. Three other families lived in this house after that, before we did."

"Would you like to read her book, Theo?" asked Laura. "You can borrow it."

Theo looked at Dan. "Yes, take it," he said. "I have several other copies upstairs. I'd still like to know what this one is doing here, though."

When they all ignored him, he retreated behind his magazine and Theo opened up *In Summer Time*.

The spongy pages smelled stale. Theo read the description of the story on the front flap of the jacket—it did look good. And its author had lived right in this house! She turned to the back flap. A blurry photograph floated above a few lines of print. "Miss Cecily Stone resides in Victoria, B.C., Canada," it said. "Besides writing for children she is an avid gardener."

Theo looked at the picture again. A gaunt woman stared back at her.

She dropped the book on the floor so hard she looked up at Dan guiltily. He hadn't noticed. Quickly she picked it up and turned around in the armchair so her back was to the family. With trembling fingers she opened the book and examined the photograph more closely.

The face was the one she had seen last night—the face of the woman walking across the street. And now Theo knew why she looked so familiar. It was the same woman who had been watching her on the ferry.

18

All Theo could think of doing to calm her churning confusion was to read the book. Maybe it would give her a clue. She turned back to the first page and began.

The story was about two children called Edward and Susan. They discovered that when they shifted their grandmother's sundial they were taken back in time. They visited Victoria in 1881 and met Emily Carr at age ten, who demanded to know who they were and why they wore such strange clothes.

That was as far as Theo got before she had to stop for dinner. Sharon arrived to pick her up and Theo got another chapter read while her aunt stayed for coffee. Then she put the book in a plastic bag and assured Dan she would take good care of it.

"You're awfully quiet this evening," said Sharon on the way home. "Just like a little mouse, the way you were when you first came. Is something wrong?"

"No," said Theo, "but could I go right to bed and read?"

Sharon laughed. "Of course! I'm so glad you're reading."

She let Theo keep her light on until nine. Theo planned to stay awake until Sharon was asleep and turn it on again, but her eyes closed with exhaustion from the night before. She woke very early and finished the book.

It was such a good story she forgot why she was reading it. She only wondered how Emily and Edward and Susan would find their way back through the forest, and if Edward and Susan would be able to return to the present. When they did, and the plot unwound to a completely satisfying conclusion, she closed it up and sighed with pleasure.

Then she remembered who had written this book. Cecily Stone. The woman she had seen crossing the street from the cemetery, the woman on the ferry who had stared at her and Rae so avidly. But Cecily Stone was dead …

A chill went through Theo; she warmed up under her covers until Sharon called her to get up.

That morning she looked for Cecily Stone's other book in the school library, but neither of her titles was there. Theo picked out two other books to take home. In the evening she asked Sharon if there was a big library in Victoria.

"There's the main branch downtown," said her aunt.

"Can I go there tomorrow after school? Please, Sharon. I'll be really careful. There's something I need to find out."

"Something for school?"

"Well … no. Just something I'm interested in." It would have been much easier to lie, but she'd promised Sharon she wouldn't.

"Wait until Saturday and I'll take you then. It will give you something to do while your friends are away."

The Kaldors were visiting their grandparents in Vancouver for Easter. Before this week Theo hadn't been able to stop thinking of how she was once supposed to go with them—before she started to fade.

Now she had forgotten they were going. All she could think about was Cecily Stone. She examined the photograph again and again until she knew the face from memory. Cecily's expression was intense and inward, as if she were thinking hard about something. She was standing in front of a tree, but Theo couldn't tell if it was the tree at the Kaldors'.

Saturday took years to come. Only reading helped the time go faster. Theo raced through six books and the school librarian began praising her as all the others had.

It poured on Good Friday. Sharon took Theo to a special mass in the morning. In the afternoon they cleaned out the kitchen cupboards. On Saturday Theo had to shop for a lot of food with Sharon before they could go to the library. Skye, Robin and Carol were coming for Easter dinner tomorrow; Theo had forgotten about that, too.

After lunch Sharon finally took her to a large building

downtown. "I'll be in the magazine department, Theo. I'll come and get you in an hour—will that be long enough for your project?"

"I hope so," said Theo. When Sharon had walked away, she looked around the library desperately. Where should she begin?

First she went to the children's department and found both novels by Cecily Stone. She examined them quickly, but they didn't have dust jackets and there was no author information inside. The one she hadn't read was called *The Huntleys of Hurley Hall*. Clutching it to her, Theo approached the children's information desk. "Excuse me."

A man looked up; he was cutting out pink paper pigs and printing names on them. "Yes?"

"Do you have any information about a writer called Cecily Stone?"

"Hmmm … she sounds familiar. Is she Canadian?"

"She lived in Victoria!" said Theo indignantly. "She wrote this book." She showed it to him.

"I'll ask the children's librarian—I'm just a clerk." He went away and returned with a glamorous-looking woman wearing lots of make-up and jewellery. "So you want to find out about our Cecily! We're rarely asked about her. I'm afraid I can't give you much information. She wasn't very well known. I'm sure she would have been if she'd lived longer, poor woman. Follow me and I'll show you what we have."

She took Theo to the adult reference section and sat her down with a file folder labelled STONE, CECILY and a fat book with a place marked in it. Theo looked at the book first; it contained short biographies of Canadian writers. There wasn't much more about Cecily than had been on the jacket flap, except for calling her "a promising writer for the young." But it was exciting to read the address of the Kaldors' house as her residence.

She opened the file. It was disappointingly thin. There were a few short reviews of the books, each complimenting the author for setting stories in British Columbia. A photocopy of a newspaper clipping announced the "untimely death of Miss Cecily Margaret Stone, daughter of the prominent Victoria lawyer, the late Mr. Giles Stone. Miss Stone was a writer of children's novels, a career she began later in life. She was a member of the Garden Society and had a special interest in heritage roses."

"It's not much, is it?" The fancy librarian was leaning over Theo, her bracelets jingling. "She didn't have any relatives and nobody published any memoirs of her. All that's left are the books. Are you doing a school project on her? I think her books are quite good, even if they are rather dated for modern kids."

"I *loved* the one I read," said Theo fiercely.

The librarian looked apologetic. "I'm glad. I bet Cecily would be happy to know that someone's still reading them. I hope you like the other one just as much."

Theo found out how to get a library card. She checked out the book and she and Sharon went home.

SHE MANAGED to get halfway through *The Huntleys of Hurley Hall* before dinner. The story took place at the turn of the century, in a large house on the Gorge in Victoria. It was about four brothers and sisters—Frank, Louise, Perry and Gwyneth—who found a secret passage.

Theo adored it. Nothing much happened, but the children seemed so happy, like the ones in the books about families she'd read in Vancouver. They had their bad times—there was an embarrassing episode when Gwyneth, Theo's favourite, fell into a pond at a birthday party—but they were such a secure, united family. Like the Kaldors …

Sharon called her to get ready; they were going to Mandy's for dinner. "Can I take my book?" asked Theo.

"You *are* reading a lot now, aren't you? I suppose so, but don't read at the table."

Theo sat impatiently through the meal. Sharon and Mandy were talking about a man at work they both had a crush on, but all Theo could think about was the Huntleys. After dinner she almost reached the end of the book while Sharon and Mandy watched a video. They got home so late that Sharon made Theo put her light out right away.

She finished the book the next morning before church,

nibbling on the large chocolate egg that had appeared beside her bed. After church she helped Sharon peel potatoes and set the table but her mind was still on the book. It was easy to tell it was by the same person who'd written *In Summer Time*. The stories were very different, but the same voice was relating them.

Reading both books hadn't helped Theo find out more about Cecily the person, just Cecily the storyteller. There was no hint in either one of the Kaldors' house or neighbourhood, or the woman who had once lived there.

Theo couldn't get Cecily's three faces out of her mind: her curious, sympathetic face on the ferry, her dreamy expression as she walked across the street and her intense look in the photograph. She knew that all three women were Cecily. It wasn't possible; but lots of things had happened this year that weren't possible. This was more magic! And somehow it seemed linked to the magic time when she had lived with the family.

All evening she brooded about Cecily. "What's wrong with you?" asked Skye, as soon as they went to Theo's room after dinner. "You act as if you're in some kind of trance or something!"

Theo blinked. "Sorry," she mumbled.

Skye set up one of the board games Sharon had bought Theo. "I never see you!" She was close to tears. "Aren't we friends any more?"

"Sure," said Theo automatically. She tried to pay

attention to the game, but Skye had to keep reminding her when it was her turn.

THEO PLAYED with Skye for most of Easter Monday. She pretended to, anyway—she was like a puppet again, part of her going through the motions, but her real self focusing on Cecily. Skye kept accusing her of not listening.

If she had magically seen Cecily two times, the only way to see her again was to go to one of the places Cecily had been. She couldn't go on the ferry; but of course she could go to the Kaldors' house.

She phoned Anna on Tuesday evening while Sharon was downstairs doing the laundry. "Hi, Theo!" said Anna. "Did you have a good Easter? We have a present from Vancouver for you. Are you coming over this Saturday?"

"Can I come for the night again?" Theo asked.

Anna sounded surprised. "I guess so. Just a minute, I'll ask Mum."

After she said it was all right, Theo waited to tell Sharon.

Her aunt put down the heavy laundry basket and looked worried. "Oh, hon, don't you think you're spending too much time over there? I know how much you like them, but you don't want to wear out your welcome—you've just *had* a sleepover. And Robin told me that Skye feels neglected. You can't forget her, you know—she's such an anxious child, she needs a friend."

Theo stiffened. "I spent all day yesterday with Skye. And the Kaldors want me to come overnight." She didn't tell Sharon she had suggested it.

Sharon sighed. "All right, then. I suppose it's up to you to choose your friends, and they *are* wonderful ones. But try not to forget about Skye."

Theo was so excited about being able to go, she kissed Sharon's cheek. "Thanks! I'll be nicer to Skye, I promise."

All week she tried. Skye was so easy to please; she revived under Theo's attention like a plant that had needed water.

Theo held tight to her secret about Cecily. Was she really going to catch a glimpse of her again? The possibility was both exciting and scary.

THEO HANDED *In Summer Time* to Dan. "Did you enjoy it?" he asked.

"It's one of the best books I've ever read!" Theo told him. "I found her other one in the library and read it, too. Do you know anything more about her?"

Dan shook his head. "She must have led a very quiet life. Writers often do—their adventures are in their books. All I know is that she once lived in this house. I can show you her grave, though. Would you like to see it?"

"Oh, yes!"

Dan smiled at her enthusiasm. "I have to go to the university for a while, but I'll show you after lunch."

Anna and Lisbeth dragged Theo upstairs to tell her about their trip to Vancouver. "John went snowboarding at Whistler with our cousins but we weren't allowed to go with them," complained Lisbeth.

"We built a fort on the beach out of driftwood but some mean kids wrecked it," said Anna.

They gave Theo a small stuffed whale they'd bought at the aquarium. Theo thanked them, but all she could think about was seeing Cecily's grave. It hadn't even occurred to her that she'd be buried across the street.

Only Anna came with Theo and Dan. They followed him along the pathway almost to the end of the cemetery. Then he led them across the grass to the edge of a hill which dropped to Dallas Road and the sea.

"It's right around the war memorial," said Dan, examining the markers. "Ah … here you are, Theo."

The grass plot was outlined by a cement rectangle. Two plaques were set in it. The shiny dark one said:

GILES WILLIAM STONE
BORN 1876 DIED 1945

PHILIPPA MAY STONE
BORN 1885 DIED 1949

The other marker was in the shape of an open book. Its letters read CECILY MARGARET STONE, 1915–1956.

Underneath the dates was a quotation: AND THE BOOKS SHALL BE OPENED.

Theo knelt and ran her fingers over the smooth marble book and the rough letters. She stood up and smiled at Dan. "Thank you for showing me."

"You're really interested in her, aren't you? I'm touched by how much you love Cecily Stone's books, Theo. John and Anna liked them too."

Theo was studying Cecily's grave again. Some of the surrounding plots were brightened with grape hyacinths or Easter lilies in pots, but this one was straggly with rough grass.

"At least Cecily has a good view!" said Dan. Anna giggled. Theo tried to memorize the plot's location as they walked away.

ONCE AGAIN Theo was lying awake while Anna and Lisbeth breathed steadily. After she heard their parents come up, she'd sit by the window again.

She yawned, her body limp with drained excitement. It wanted to give in to sleep but Theo struggled to keep her eyes open.

But when she opened them next, she knew the night was almost over. She jumped up angrily and darted to the window. It was almost dawn; she could see the hedge across the street in the thin light. One bird had begun a hesitant morning call.

She'd missed her! Theo watched for a few minutes but no gliding woman appeared. She almost began to cry. Then she was riveted by an idea.

Why not go out? Cecily had come from the cemetery last time—maybe she was there. Maybe she was by her own grave! Theo didn't stop to think of what that might imply. She picked up her shoes and crept downstairs.

In the hall she put on her jacket over her pyjamas and did up her shoes. Bingo came lumbering out of the kitchen, stretching as he walked. "Is it morning already?" his puzzled brown eyes asked her.

Theo hesitated. She'd feel safer with Bingo along, but what if he barked? She made him sit while she opened and closed the door as softly as she could. Standing on the front steps, she took a deep breath. After all, it was almost morning; Anna and John had once sneaked out at night. If someone saw her, she could just say she felt like going for a walk.

Her legs still trembled as she went slowly along the same route Dan had taken her this afternoon. What was she going to find? The closer she came, the more she wanted to turn back; but something compelled her to keep walking.

When she reached Cecily's grave, it was deserted. Theo was both relieved and disappointed. She stood there a long time, the only sounds the increasing bird chorus and the rhythmic lap of the sea below.

Theo turned to face the war memorial—and froze. She tried to scream but it came out as a muffled choke.

A woman was sitting on the lowest step of the memorial. When she heard Theo, she jumped up with astonished delight. "Can you really see me?" asked Cecily Stone.

19

"Don't be afraid," said Cecily. "I won't hurt you."

"But you're—you're—"

"I'm dead. That's what the gravestone says, doesn't it? My body is buried there. *It's* gone. But the rest of me is still alive."

Theo's voice finally worked properly. "Then you're a ghost," she shuddered. She tried to make her legs run away, but they were rubber.

"I suppose so, although I prefer the word 'spirit' to 'ghost.' But there you are, I'm just being particular about words as usual." Her expression was yearning. "You're the first person who has ever seen me—imagine that! I haven't talked to a living soul for forty years! Why don't you come and sit down, Theo?"

She didn't look like a ghost. She wasn't transparent or white or any of the ways ghosts looked in movies or comics.

Cecily looked exactly the same as she had the last

two times. She was wearing the same pants and baggy coat, her hair was still messy and her eyes were still sad. Theo's skin crawled with fear, but she couldn't help feeling curious and excited as well. She stayed where she was, but she dropped to the grass, clutching her trembling legs.

"How do you know my name?" she whispered.

Cecily sat down on the step and smiled. "I heard your mother call you Theo on the ferry. It's a good, strong name—it has a real ring of individuality to it."

"I saw you watching us."

"You saw me there as well? I wondered, because you kept looking at me, but I wasn't sure. If you could see me I apologize for staring at you like that. I often travel on the ferry and watch people. It used to be my best place for getting ideas."

"Ideas?"

"Ideas for books. I was a writer." Her expression became even sadder.

"I know," said Theo. "I've read both of your books."

"I hoped you would. That's why I put one where you'd find it." Cecily looked eager. "Did you—what did you think of them?"

Theo stopped trembling. "I *loved* them! My favourite characters were Edward and Gwyneth."

"I'm so glad," said Cecily warmly. "That's the best part of writing—hearing the reaction of my readers. Or at least, that *was* the best part."

She stood up and paced the grass. Theo tried to keep still. When Cecily moved, she did seem like a ghost. Her feet hovered slightly over the grass instead of touching it.

"You can't imagine how utterly *frustrating* it is, Theo, to be cut off from your vocation in the middle of it! There were so many books I wanted to write! My head was bursting with ideas, especially since I started so late. And then to *die*. To die at age forty-one, just when I had begun to master my craft!"

"I'm sorry," whispered Theo.

"If only I hadn't waited so long to start," continued Cecily. "I always wanted to write, but I didn't have much confidence in myself and it certainly wasn't something my parents would have approved of. When Father died, I looked after Mother for four years. After her death I changed my whole life." Her face lost some of its anguish. "There wasn't much money—my parents weren't rich, although they took care to associate with people who were. But I was left the house and enough to live on. First I sold all my fancy clothes. Mother had always dressed me, even as an adult. I only wore comfortable slacks after that—I've never given a hoot about clothes. Then I finally got started on my first book. What a relief it was! All I did those last years was write and garden—I was perfectly happy. Until I began to feel sick …"

"Couldn't you still write?" asked Theo timidly. Then

she felt her face redden. "I'm sorry—that was a stupid question."

"It's not stupid," said Cecily sadly. "I tried. I went into my house and found a pen and tried to write words on paper—but the paper was blank. That was my most despairing moment, looking down and seeing that paper full of nothing." She sighed deeply. "I can still read, at least. I've read most of the books the families who've lived in my house have owned. The Kaldors have the best collection."

Theo smiled—so that's why Dan's books were always misplaced! Smiling made her braver. She tried to ask Cecily what she most wanted to know—but the question was so hard to put into words.

"Why … why are you here?" she whispered.

Cecily understood at once. "You mean why haven't I really died? Why am I not at rest, as I should be?" She sighed again. "It's because I haven't written the book I was meant to write. The first two were perfectly adequate—but they weren't *me*, they weren't my story. All the time I was ill a new idea was forming in my mind. I knew it would be my best book."

"What was it?"

"It was about being a lonely child. Being an outcast and yearning for a different kind of life. All the children in my books were so happy, so confident. They hadn't much inner life. I wanted to write about a child who was true to the child I once was."

Cecily began pacing again. "I couldn't flesh it out, though. I wanted the story to be a fantasy and set in the present time, since I'd written so much about the past. I needed to find a real, modern child to trigger it— someone to inspire me to turn my glimmerings of an idea into a solid story with a beginning, a middle and an end. I looked for that child for years. Every once in a while I'd travel on the ferry and look there. And it gave me something to do. I'd simply go back and forth on the ferry from Victoria to Vancouver, sometimes for months. The last time I did that I saw—"

"You saw me," breathed Theo.

"Yes!" Cecily looked excited. "I saw you and your mother and I moved closer to listen."

Theo remembered that terrible argument. Some of the anger she'd felt when she'd first noticed Cecily returned. "I don't think it's polite to listen to other people's conversations," she said. Then she shrank at her boldness.

But Cecily laughed. "You're absolutely right. It's very rude—but I've always done it. I'm incurably nosy. And as soon as I started listening I knew I finally had my story."

"What was it?" whispered Theo.

"I noticed how unhappy and lost you seemed, and I knew from your conversation that you were going to Victoria to live with your aunt—and that you didn't want to."

"No," whispered Theo.

"You also looked so dreamy—as if you were off in another world. You were making something up, weren't you? Fantasizing."

"Yes," said Theo. "I always did, then."

Cecily clapped her hands. "I knew it! I did exactly the same when I was a child. My parents were very correct and cold. I was lonely but I led a vivid fantasy life inside. When I grew up I turned my fantasies into stories. You're supposed to stop pretending when you're an adult—but some of us never do."

Theo wished she'd go back to *her*—to Cecily's idea about her.

"I'm digressing, aren't I? As I was saying, watching you gave me the clue to my story. I thought that you needed a proper family. There's a family that I've watched a lot. You know them. They live in my house."

"The Kaldors!"

"Yes. John and Anna and Lisbeth and Ben. I've enjoyed observing their antics and listening to their conversations over the years—they often play in here. I've always been drawn to large, happy families, since my own was neither. So I decided you were probably fantasizing about being in such a family—and then you found one!"

Theo couldn't speak. She listened tensely, half-guessing what Cecily would say next.

"In my story you would meet the Kaldors on the ferry

and play with them. I knew the sorts of things they did, since they were once on the ferry when I was. Then you'd make a wish on the new moon and be in the family. While you were there you'd be healed. It was going to be a very *satisfying* story. And I'd set it here—in my childhood home and neighbourhood."

The excitement left Cecily's face. "The trouble is, I couldn't work out the dynamics in my head. It was easy to imagine all the things you'd do while you lived with them—how they'd buy you clothes, how secure and loved you would become. But there were so many flaws. The transition to the family was too easy. It wasn't believable that you'd just wish for something and get it. Your time there was too happy. There wasn't enough conflict, although I tried to create some in an incident when you got into trouble for going downtown. And I couldn't figure out what happened to your mother, or how—or if—you'd go back to her."

Cecily gazed at the sea. "It was the story I'd wanted to write all my life. You seemed so much like me as a child. I recognized your *yearning* so much."

When she turned around, her expression was despairing. "But it was just an idea! It was only in my head. It will never be a real book. I could have worked it out on paper. It would have changed a lot if I'd been able to write it down. But of course I can never do that."

Theo had trouble breathing. "Cecily …" she croaked. She stood up and faced her. "Your idea *did* work. I did go into the family."

"Whatever do you mean?"

"Everything happened just like you said! I was always thinking about families, ones with four children and a mother and father. And I met the Kaldors on the ferry and they were perfect—exactly what I wanted!"

Cecily looked astonished. "They were on the ferry? You talked to them?"

"Yes! I wished I could live with them and I did! I belonged to their family until Easter. It was wonderful. The most wonderful thing that's ever happened to me! But then I started not to be there … to sort of fade … and then I was back on the ferry with Rae."

"Well, I'll be … that's incredible, Theo! It's hard to believe."

It was hard to believe she was standing in the cemetery talking to a ghost, too, thought Theo.

"But how did it happen?" she asked.

"I don't know. There's no point in trying to explain these things," Cecily said slowly. "I think your time with the Kaldors must have been a combination of both of our fantasies—mine and yours."

"It *did* seem weird that I just wished to be there, and that they accepted me so easily. I couldn't decide if it was a dream or magic," said Theo.

Cecily mused on this. "I think it was both. An idea is like a dream—a dream of what could be. Your fantasy of being in a family was a dream—a wish, a daydream. And stories *are* magic. I'm so glad it happened, Theo, that you really belonged to such a special family for a while."

"But I couldn't *stay*!" burst out Theo. That seemed Cecily's fault.

"No … You faded away just as my idea faded away—when I couldn't solve the main problem of the story, that your time in the family was too perfect. Real life isn't perfect, and good fiction has to *seem* like real life."

"I liked it being perfect!" protested Theo.

"But you found the Kaldors again, didn't you?"

"Yes, but it's not the same! They aren't perfect any more and I don't belong to them—I'm just their friend, not their sister."

"Friends are very valuable," said Cecily. "Like gold. I never had many—you're lucky. I was so surprised to see you with those four children, Theo. To see *you* again! I watched you playing here with them and I saw you looking out of the window of their house last week."

"I saw you, too," whispered Theo. "Did you cover me up?"

"Yes," said Cecily gently. "I don't usually go upstairs, but I couldn't resist getting a longer look at you. Then I wished you could read my books, so I put one in the living-room."

They exchanged smiles. But then Theo glanced at the plot and shivered as she tried to reconcile Cecily being buried there and Cecily sitting across from her.

"Are there other ghosts here?" she asked in a wavery voice.

"I haven't seen any. It's a myth that cemeteries are full of ghosts. If people linger on after they die, they linger in the places that meant the most to them. But this was my place. I came here every day of my life. At the end of it, it soothed me to know I'd be buried here."

She stood up and beckoned Theo over to her grave. "Do you like my inscription? I left instructions for it in my will. An open book ... that's all that will save us, I think."

Sometimes Cecily was hard to understand. "Save who—from what?" asked Theo.

"I think an open book symbolizes imagination. Only imagination will save people from their narrow, cramped expectations of life—like those my parents had." She chuckled. "But enough of my philosophizing. When you've done nothing but *think* for forty years you get pretty pedantic."

They stood there in silence, Theo as close to Cecily as she dared. Something told her it wouldn't be right to touch her.

Beyond the plot brilliant yellow broom tumbled down the bank. The warming sun drew out its bitter odour.

"I should go back," said Theo. "They'll wonder where I am."

"I'll come part of the way with you," said Cecily. She glided beside Theo as far as the entrance, her feet making no sound on the pavement. Theo's shadow stretched in front of her in the slanting morning light—but Cecily had no shadow.

Theo turned at the hedge. "Will I see you again?"

"I don't know," said Cecily. "I hope so. Perhaps you will if you really need to." She smiled sadly. "I'm not sure how long I'll be here now, Theo. I found the story I was looking for—and I'm so amazed and delighted that it touched you. Now there's only one more thing I need to find." She looked intently at Theo. "It's been extremely pleasant talking to you, dear child. Thank you for listening. Go on now, before the Kaldors get up."

"Goodbye," whispered Theo. She ran across the street, then she turned around to wave. But Cecily had gone.

20

Theo sat in a daze at breakfast. She had got back just in time to slip into bed before Ben wandered in and ordered someone to give him some cereal.

Had the incredible time she'd just spent been a dream? Had Cecily been a dream? Theo could still hear the angular woman's musical voice and see her long hands emphasize her words as she talked. She knew she'd been real.

Well, not *real* ... a ghost. A ghost writer! Theo told herself gleefully.

She yawned for the rest of the day, glad that Dan took them to a movie and she didn't have to talk much. She had no idea what the movie was about. She went over and over Cecily's conversation, trying to remember every word.

When she said goodbye after dinner, she surprised the family by giving each of them a hug. The Kaldors seemed like characters that Cecily had created. Of course they were real—more real now than they had been in that magic time. But if it wasn't for Cecily, Theo would never have met them.

Late that night the apartment buzzer wakened Theo. She heard Sharon struggle out of bed to answer it. "Who is it? Oh! Come right up!"

The light went on in the living-room. Theo floated in and out of sleep as the door opened and someone came in. "You're soaked!" she heard Sharon say. There were whispers and shushes and quick footsteps. Theo sat up as Sharon began to close her door. "I'm awake."

"You are? Then you may as well get up. It's your mother."

"Hi, kid," said Rae. She was rubbing her hair with a towel. Her bare feet were red; sopping socks were heaped beside them. Her backpack and a battered suitcase stood by the door.

"I'll make some cocoa," said Sharon. She began heating up milk while Theo continued to stand and stare at her mother. When Rae babbled about how hard it was raining, Theo sat down beside her aunt, as far away from Rae as she could get.

"I'm glad you've finally come to visit, Mary Rae," said Sharon, her voice chilly. "We haven't heard from you for so long."

Rae looked at them, her wet curls making her head look small. "I've left Cal," she said bluntly. "I had nowhere to live so I quit my job and came here."

Sharon looked shaken. "Oh ... but the last ferry gets in at 10:30. Where have you been all this time?"

"I wasn't sure you'd want me. So I sat in a restaurant on Douglas Street until it closed, then I walked over. Can I stay for a while?"

Some of Sharon's coldness melted. "You shouldn't wander around alone at this time of night—it's dangerous! Of course you can stay."

Rae fumbled with her cigarette package. "I'm not living with that *pig* any more. I can't believe I ever saw anything in him."

Sharon glanced at Theo. "We can talk about it later. You go back to bed, Theo. I'll get out the foamie." Her voice was exhausted.

Theo tried to listen to Rae and Sharon through the closed door, but all she could hear was the roll of foam being dragged out of the cupboard, then silence.

Rae. How long was she going to stay? Would she make Theo go back to Vancouver with her? Angry tears began to slip down Theo's face. Just as she'd found the Kaldors— just as she'd found *Cecily*—her mother had to come along and spoil everything.

CAL HAD STARTED DRINKING too much; that was all Theo knew. Rae would have told her more, but Sharon stopped her every time she tried. "That's not suitable for a child to hear," she said. Theo was grateful; she didn't want to hear more. She shut her ears to the long whispered conversations Rae and Sharon had after she was in bed.

The only thing she wanted to know was how long Rae was going to stay. Every day Theo and Sharon arrived home to find the apartment filled with smoke and Rae sprawled in front of the TV. They waited tensely for her to tell them her plans. Sharon acted more and more irritated with her sister. She no longer tried to please her, as she had when Rae had first brought Theo here.

On Friday they were sitting on the couch after dinner when Sharon stood up and switched off the TV. "What are you going to *do*, Mary Rae? You can't stay here forever. This apartment is too small for three people."

Rae looked apologetic. "I know, I know. Just give me a bit more time."

"Do you want to talk to a counsellor? Karen at work knows someone who—"

Rae took out a cigarette. "I'll figure this out on my own, okay?"

Sharon took a deep breath. "You don't seem to be figuring anything out! All you do is watch TV and smoke. I've been figuring some things out, Mary Rae. From now on I want you to only smoke on the balcony. It's not good for Theo to breathe secondhand smoke. And while you're here I think you should pick her up at school every day. It would save me the cost of after-school day care." Her voice became even shriller. "And you could contribute something for food. You must have *some* money. Don't you realize I've been supporting your child all this time?"

She sat down beside Theo and gave her a hug. "It's not that I haven't enjoyed it. I've come to love Theo very much. But you said you'd send money and you haven't once! I've had to use my savings, and they're almost gone!"

Rae looked trapped. "You can really speak your mind when you want to, can't you?" she muttered. She jerked her unlit cigarette in and out of her mouth. "You're right, of course. I've been a shit about everything, haven't I? Okay, it's a deal. I'll only smoke outside. I'll pick up the kid after school and I'll give you some money when my unemployment cheque comes. But I can't tell you how long I'm staying—I just don't know yet."

Then Sharon asked the question Theo dreaded. "But what about your *child*? You have to decide what you're going to do about her! I really think you should talk to someone, Mary Rae."

Rae stood up and headed for the balcony. "Just give me some time, won't you? I'm not going to see any damn counsellor. I've had enough people poking their noses into my business."

"Don't use that kind of language in front of Theo," said Sharon quietly.

Rae laughed as she opened the door to the balcony. "Theo's heard a lot worse than that, haven't you, kid?"

THEO COULD HARDLY WAIT to escape to the Kaldors the next day. She paced impatiently while Sharon searched for her keys.

"Who *are* these people?" asked Rae.

"They're a wonderful family that Theo's met," said Sharon. "She's been visiting them almost every Saturday. The mother's an artist and the father's an English professor."

"They sound pretty uppity," said Rae.

"They're not!" cried Theo. "They're nice!" It was the first time she'd spoken directly to her mother since she'd come.

"Okay, okay. They're your friends. But why do you go there every week?"

"Because I *like* them!" retorted Theo. She flounced after Sharon, slamming the door on Rae.

She'd hoped to forget about her mother at the Kaldors but it didn't work. She couldn't enjoy herself, knowing Rae would still be there when she went back.

When they were playing in the cemetery, Theo led the others to Cecily's grave and lingered there longingly.

"But we saw this last week," complained Anna. "Come on, Theo, let's play hide-and-seek."

Theo stayed behind. If only Cecily would appear again! "Cecily," she whispered, but nothing happened and finally she ran after the others.

"Is something wrong, Theo?" asked Anna, when they

had collapsed under the angel after the game. "You seem so sad."

"My mother's here," said Theo.

"Oh!" Anna looked surprised. "Is that ... okay?"

But Theo just shrugged, wishing she hadn't said anything. She thought of Rae compared to Laura—Laura who had once been her mother, but only in a fantasy; that is, an *idea* for a fantasy that had faded away ... Rolling over, she began to yank up grass and throw it away.

WHEN THEO CAME OUT of school at three she flushed with embarrassment. Rae was standing by the fence, dressed in shiny leggings and a skimpy T-shirt that didn't reach her waist. A cigarette dangled from her fingers. None of the other kids' mothers looked like a teenager. Theo tried to rush Rae away as fast as possible.

"The old place hasn't changed much," said Rae. "Boy, did they hate me there!"

Theo didn't answer.

"I hear Sharon drags you to church every Sunday. You don't have to go with her."

"I like it," said Theo. "It's peaceful there."

Rae shrugged. "Suit yourself. But I think Sharon's been coddling you. There's no need to pick you up from school every day as if you were five. It's only a few blocks. You could walk home by yourself."

Theo didn't answer. She *would* rather go home on her own but she didn't want Rae to know she agreed with her.

"It's strange to be in this neighbourhood again. Do you want to see the house I grew up in?"

"Sharon already showed it to me," said Theo, but Rae was walking in that direction.

"They've sure spiffed it up," said Rae when they reached the blue cottage. "See that big tree by the window? That's how I used to sneak out at night. Sharon saw me once and snitched. She was such a saint. Dad never yelled at *her*." She stubbed out her cigarette and lit another one. "The good sister and the bad sister—that was us. Sharon would eat all her vegetables. I'd pretend to be sick and spit them into the toilet."

"Why?"

Rae looked surprised. "Why? I guess because they *expected* me to be bad. Ma would laugh and call me her wild one, and Dad would just get angry. He had no time for me—he liked Sharon the best. They would spend hours looking at books about other countries and shut me out completely. It wasn't fair! Are you listening to me, Theo?"

As usual Rae was like a child wanting attention. "Sharon says there's no point in wishing the past was different," Theo told her. "It's all water under the bridge."

She sighed and took her mother's hand. "Come on, let's go home."

Rae told Sharon that Theo could go to Skye's house by herself and even play in Beacon Hill Park with her.

"But that's not safe!" said Sharon. "What if they meet a stranger?"

Rae laughed. "Theo can look after herself. If she can survive downtown Vancouver, she sure isn't going to have a problem in Victoria."

"But what about that little boy who disappeared?"

"That was a tragedy. But look, Sharon, nothing's safe. You never let the kid out of your sight! Theo knows how to deal with strangers and she and Skye can watch out for each other. Don't you remember all the days we used to spend in the park?"

"Yes, but those were different times," said Sharon.

"Not that different. And I think Theo should be allowed to walk back and forth to school with Skye. She wants to, don't you, kid? She's embarrassed to be picked up like a baby."

"Do you want that, Theo?" asked Sharon. In spite of her disappointed expression Theo had to nod.

"But—" Then Sharon looked resigned. "All right. She's your child, after all. As long as you're here after school."

"I'm so glad you're my friend again," said Skye. Theo enjoyed her more now that there was some space around them. They walked back and forth to school every day with a gang of other kids on their street—Darcy and his little sister Madison, Simran, Alan, and the Kwon twins.

After school they had a snack at Skye's or Theo's, then went out again to the park. Rae had persuaded Sharon to buy Theo a secondhand bike, promising to pay her back. They rode their bikes along the cement walkways, stopping to feed the ducks or gaze at the petting zoo. They had strict instructions about never leaving the paths, but Theo felt much freer. That was because of Rae, she had to admit.

Skye didn't go on and on about her father as much. She was cheerful and relaxed. She's happy because I'm her friend, Theo realized. It felt powerful to make someone happier.

Skye accepted that Theo still abandoned her every Saturday to go to the Kaldors. Now she waited eagerly each Sunday afternoon to hear what Theo had done with them.

Laura kept sugggesting that Theo invite her mother for dinner, but every time she did, Theo made up an excuse. As long as she kept everything in separate boxes—Sharon and Rae, school and Skye, and the Kaldors on Saturdays—she could cope.

Spring was at its ripest. The Kaldors' garden was thick with rhododendrons and the first fat peonies were opening. Dan told Theo that much of the garden had been planted by Cecily Stone. "Wait until you see her roses," he said. "We have some of the oldest species in the city."

Theo always encouraged him to talk about Cecily. "What does 'out of print' mean?" she asked.

"It means that no more copies of Cecily Stone's books will ever be published. The only ones left are those that already exist. That's why I collect them. Once I found both titles in a garage sale."

Theo thought sadly of Cecily's only two books being rejected in a garage sale or sitting unread on the shelf of the public library.

She hung around Cecily's grave as much as she could. Often she called her name, but the ghost didn't appear. Theo almost cried when she thought of never seeing Cecily again. Had she gone away for good, as she'd hinted at?

The warm days drifted by. Rae and Sharon circled each other with increasing tension in the crowded apartment. Theo knew that something was about to explode between them, that this fragile limbo couldn't last. Often Sharon went out on mysterious errands. She didn't say where she was going, but Theo was sure she was just trying to avoid Rae.

It wasn't as easy for Theo. She had to spend endless evenings sitting in front of the TV with her mother. Sometimes she'd look up in a panic, afraid she was back in Vancouver.

Rae left the room often to puff and pace on the balcony. She must be trying to decide what to do. Then what would happen to Theo?

21

Rae broke the silence first. "I want to talk to you, Sharon," she said one evening in her sweetest voice.

"Okay," said Sharon warily. "But if it's about Theo, I don't think she should listen."

"Whatever you say," said Rae. "Why don't you go for a ride on your bike, kid?"

"Not on her own! Theo, honey, would you mind going down the hall and having a visit with Tara while your mother and I talk? I just saw her come in."

Theo slid out of the apartment but after she closed the door she opened it a crack and crouched by it. She wasn't going to miss hearing them decide her future. She heard her mother and her aunt pull up chairs at the kitchen table.

"I've been thinking about you, Shar," began Rae. "You've really been great these past months. You've done so much for Theo and she obviously likes you. Thanks for everything."

"You're welcome," said Sharon suspiciously.

"You like Theo, don't you?"

"I adore her! You know that."

"She likes Victoria, too, much more than she liked Vancouver. She has friends here and she's doing much better in school. The trouble is, I don't like Victoria. It's as boring as it was when I lived here. I miss the big city a lot and I've decided to go back."

"But—"

"Let me finish, please." Rae's voice was strained. "I don't think it would be fair to take Theo with me. You're a much better mother to her than I am. I know I was bad about sending you money before, but if I promise to send you some regularly this time—if we put it in writing— would you keep looking after her? At least until she finishes elementary school?" Her voice became cajoling again. "Don't you think it would be a shame to yank her out of a place she likes?"

Theo heard Sharon breathe heavily—as heavily as she herself was breathing.

Please say yes, she begged.

Then she jumped as Sharon banged her hand on the table. "That does it! Do you think you can just dump your child on people until it's convenient for you to have her again? You listen to me, Mary Rae. *I've* been thinking, too—and making plans, since you seem incapable of that. I've been to a counsellor and I've been talking to Father

Wilson at the church. Much as I love Theo, I can't take care of her any longer. She's not my child—she's yours. She *needs* you. She needs you to be a real mother to her. So here's my plan. Father Wilson knows a woman in the parish who wants someone to live in her basement suite. She'd charge a low rent in exchange for taking care of the house and her dogs when she's away. Apparently she travels a lot. I've been to see the place—it's very bright and has a separate entrance into the garden. And it's just a few blocks away! I'm sure you could find some sort of job in the tourist stores downtown. Theo and I could still see a lot of each other and she could keep going to the same school."

"You've got to be kidding," said Rae. "You've organized my whole life nicely, haven't you? Sorry, Sharon, but I'm going back to Vancouver. If you don't want Theo, I'll have to take her with me."

"I won't let you," said Sharon steadily. "You're not a good enough mother to be entirely on your own. You said yourself she needs the stability of staying here. I can't take care of her but I want her in my life. I want to make sure she's okay."

"In other words, you want to check up on me."

"Yes!" Then Sharon's voice became softer. "You need help, Mary Rae—what's wrong with that? I'd be happy to help you. But I have to lead my own life as well. I want to travel, to do things in the evenings and weekends, not to be tied down with a child."

"What if I don't want to be tied down either?"

Sharon slapped the table again. She started yelling. "Mary Rae Caffrey, when are you going to get it into your empty head that you have no choice? She's *your child*! You chose to have her and you have to take care of her! When are you going to grow up?" She began sobbing wildly.

Theo couldn't stay to hear any more. She ran down the hall and unlocked her bike from the stairwell at the end of it. Bumping it down the stairs she pushed it outside and pedalled furiously to the only person in the world she wanted to be with.

When she reached the cemetery, her heart was pounding so painfully she had to walk her bike with one hand and clutch her chest with the other. Finally she came to the far end. She crashed down her bike and ran over to the gravestone shaped like a book.

"Cecily!" she sobbed. "Cecily, where are you? I *need* you!"

"I'm coming," said the calm voice. "Can you see me? What's the matter, Theo?"

Cecily was walking towards her, deep sympathy in her eyes.

"You're still here!" choked Theo. "I'm so glad I can see you!" She tried to swallow her tears.

"I'm delighted to see you again, too." Cecily smiled.

241

"Although I *have* seen you lots of times lately. I watched you all playing hide-and-seek here last week. But tell me why you're crying so hard! No one should cry like this."

Theo squatted on the grass. "They don't w-want me."

"What do you mean?"

"Rae and Sharon. I heard them talking. Rae wants to go back to Vancouver without me and—" she shuddered "—and even *Sharon* doesn't want me! Rae asked her to keep me and she said no."

Cecily's voice sounded tearful too. "You poor, dear child."

"Couldn't you have that idea for a story again?" begged Theo. "Couldn't you put me back with the Kaldors? *Please …*"

Cecily shook her head. "It wouldn't work, Theo. It was just a fantasy that somehow became real—for you, at least. But it didn't last and it would be impossible for it to happen again. You can't live in a fantasy—you have to live the life you have."

"But what will happen to me?"

"I don't know. I feel for you deeply—it's appalling that they're juggling you around like this. But they'll decide something—they won't abandon you. I know it's difficult, but when you're young you have to cope the best you can with what adults do with your life. But remember, they can only control your outer life. Your inner life—your core—is still your own. And when you grow up, you can control all your life." She paused. "What do you *think* is going to happen?"

"I'll probably live with Rae," said Theo tightly. "She'll probably take me back to Vancouver with her."

"I'm sorry," said Cecily. "Your mother has a lot of growing up to do—I could see that on the ferry."

"I hate her!" Theo started to cry again, but more softly.

"You're allowed to feel that. But you'll just have to put up with her, unless you want to go to a foster home."

"No," shuddered Theo. "But I'll have to leave Victoria! And the Kaldors and Sharon and Skye …"

"Theo, I wish I could stop that happening, but I can't!"

Theo felt betrayed. "It's not fair! Why do some people have proper families and some don't?"

"It isn't fair at all," said Cecily. "But lots of things in life aren't fair." She sat down on the edge of her plot. "Now listen to me, Theo. I *can* give you some hope. I think you have it in you to survive all this. I think you're special. You could be what I was—a writer."

"A writer?" said Theo, astonished out of her anger.

"Yes! I've been thinking about this ever since our last conversation. You observe things, you make things up, you read, you're very intelligent and sensitive. And even though you have a difficult life, that's material!"

"Material? You mean cloth?"

Cecily threw back her head and laughed so hard that

tears ran down her cheeks. "Oh, Theo, forgive me—I keep forgetting how young you are. Material is what a writer calls the—the *stuff*, the ingredients for a good story. Your life may have been awful and it may become awful again. But it makes a much better story than the Kaldors' easy life. Do you understand?"

Theo's head was spinning. "No, I don't."

"You will one day. But for now just keep observing the richness you have—Vancouver and Victoria, your mother and your aunt, the Kaldors … Watch it, *use* it. The bad times and the good times, too. If you watch carefully, there are always what I call shining moments, even in hard times—moments of sheer joy, when you're just glad to be alive."

"*Every* moment was like that when I lived with the Kaldors," said Theo sadly.

"I'm glad I was somehow able to give you that time. It will strengthen you, remembering it." Cecily looked intently at Theo. "There's so much I want to tell you before—" She sighed and continued. "Here's what I think, Theo. Writers are both awake and dreaming. They have to pay attention—to be mindful to all the small things in life, the *details*, whether ordinary or wonderful or terrible. Then they dream of what they can turn those details into. And if your life gets really difficult, Theo, there are two things you can do. You can force yourself to see people at a distance, like someone in a story. Then they'll lose their power over you. Or you can make up something better and escape to it."

"I used to do that," said Theo.

"You can do it again. When you grow up you'll have a *treasure* of stuff—of material—to shape and transform into fiction." She sounded envious.

Theo was trying to digest her words. A writer? Her? Like Cecily? Like Arthur Ransome and E.B. White and Frances Hodgson Burnett and all the other authors she'd loved so much? A flame of excitement licked her insides.

"There's something else, Theo," said Cecily. She stood up. "It's something painful, but I have to tell you. It's time for me to move on."

"Move on?"

"Move on to the next stage—whatever that may be. I've been here for long enough—forty years! If my body were still alive I'd be eighty-one. That's long enough for anyone to hang onto life, even if it's only been a thread of life for half of it. *You* need to wake up to life—I need to go to sleep for good. There's no reason for me to linger any longer. Yes, I found the story I wanted to write. But I need to be alive to do it—to be awake. You *are* alive. Maybe you'll even write down my story someday—our story." She turned towards the sea. "I need to give it *all* up now."

Theo scrambled to her feet. "You mean you have to die? *No*, Cecily!"

"My body is already gone," Cecily reminded her. "It's time for the rest of me to go."

Theo shivered. "But aren't you scared?"

"I gave up being scared of death forty years ago, Theo," said Cecily softly. "But I don't want *you* to be frightened. Let's not talk about that any more. I want you to go home to your mother and your aunt and try to bravely accept what they've decided. One day you're going to create something wonderful. I can *feel* it. You can carry on for me. That's what I had to make sure of before I left. And Theo ..." Theo lifted her tear-stained face. "There's a small task you can do for me after I leave."

Theo tried to pay attention to Cecily's instructions. Then Cecily gazed at her tenderly, her eyes brimming. "I'm going away now, dear child. Don't forget what I've told you."

"*Cecily!*" Theo ran over and threw her arms around Cecily—but she was clinging to air.

"Cecily ..." she sobbed. "Oh, Cecily, please come back!" She flung herself in front of the grave, her tears running into the grass.

Finally she sat up and clutched her knees. She had rushed out without a jacket and the air was misty and dank. The foghorn's distant note sounded as solitary as she was.

Where should she go? She could trudge up the street to the Kaldors. They would welcome her warmly, but she couldn't bear their concern and worry. She had no one. Not Cecily, not the Kaldors, and certainly not Rae or Sharon.

Just herself … like the Cat walking by his "wild lone" …

Theo stood up and wiped the tears off her face. She picked up her bike and rode slowly back to Sharon's, thinking hard all the way.

RAE WAS ALONE in the apartment. "Hi, kid," she said wearily as Theo slumped in the couch beside her. "Did you have a good time at Tara's?"

"Where's Sharon?"

"She went over to Mandy's. We had a terrible argument. I've never seen her so angry! She said some awful things to me." Rae sniffed, and blew her nose.

Theo switched off the TV. "I was listening to you outside the door. I think everything Sharon said was right. She *shouldn't* have to live with me—she's my aunt, not my mother. You have to live with *me*."

"I know that, Theo. We'll leave Sharon alone and go back to Vancouver tomorrow." She looked exhausted. "We may have to live at the shelter until I can find another job."

"No!" Theo stood in front of her mother with clenched fists. "I'm not leaving Victoria! I like it. Sharon's found us a place to live and you can look for a job here!"

"Oh, kid, I know you like Victoria, but I don't!"

"I don't care," said Theo. "I'm more important. When I'm old enough to live on my own, you can do what you want. Right now you have to do what's best for *me*."

Rae looked astounded. "What's got into you and Sharon tonight?"

She went into the kitchen and filled a glass from the tap. "You're both picking on me," she whined. "It's not that easy to find a job, you know."

Theo sat down again and waited. Rae drank her water. She came back to the living-room. "What would I *do* here? All my old friends have left. And this city has never been my style. Most of the people are so old. 'The city of the living dead,' that's what they used to call it."

Theo kept waiting. Rae went to the bathroom and stayed there for a long time. Finally she returned and sat down on the couch beside Theo.

"I suppose … I could give it a try. I'm too tired to argue with you." She sighed. "I'll start job-hunting tomorrow."

The energy drained out of Theo. "Thanks," she mumbled.

Then, to her wonder, Rae looked abashed. "But are you sure—are you sure you *want* to live with me, Kitten? I've been a truly lousy mother! I probably should have given you up for adoption, like everyone said I should."

"Why didn't you?" whispered Theo.

"Because I wanted you. For a selfish reason—I thought

you'd give some meaning to my life. But …" Rae looked ashamed. "Babies are so scary. I didn't know what to do with you, you were so tiny and delicate—you looked breakable. And Ma and Sharon took over anyway—they knew what to do with babies. I just seemed to be in the way. So I went to live in Vancouver. I was only sixteen, remember."

Sixteen … six years older than *she* was. Theo swallowed. "Why did you take me back, then?"

"It was on one of my visits. I did visit sometimes. And you were such a neat kid! So pretty and smart and independent. You loved listening to books and you were so good—you'd play by yourself for hours. And you seemed to like me—you sat on my knee and told me funny stories about your doll. I thought it would be fun to have you again, especially since all that baby stuff—diapers and bottles and mushy food—was over. So I took you back to Vancouver. Ma and Sharon were furious. They threatened to try to get custody of you, to say I was an unfit mother. So I moved and never gave them my address."

Rae sighed. "But it didn't work out the way I thought it would. I could never get a good job and then I had another mouth to feed. And you didn't seem to like me the way you did when I was just a visitor. You screamed all the way to the ferry—everyone on the bus glared at me. You dug your nails into me like a fierce little wildcat—that's why I started calling you Kitten. You talked about Ma and Sharon for months. Before Ma died, I used to phone and let you talk to her, but that made you retreat from me even more. You can imagine how that made me feel."

"I'm sorry," whispered Theo.

Rae sat up straighter. "Sorry! It wasn't your fault! I shouldn't have taken you! I made a mess of both our lives."

"It wasn't all bad," Theo said quietly. "There was the time we spent the summer at the children's camp, when you had that job washing dishes. We lived in a tent and we watched the otters playing by the sea. That was fun."

Rae sighed again. "Yeah, it was. But there was never *much* fun, was there? It's great of you to say that, Kitten, but you may as well admit it—I've really botched it." She lit a cigarette and Theo didn't say a word about going onto the balcony.

"I'm not sure you *should* live with me, Theo. I don't think I'm good for you. I bet Sharon would take you if *you* asked her to."

She looked so helpless and so weak.

"Would you—would you still hit me?" said Theo. "It's *wrong* to hit children," she added firmly, remembering Anna's words.

Rae broke down in noisy, gulping sobs. "Oh, Kitten … oh, Theo … I promise I'll never, ever hit you again!"

Theo reached out one hand and smoothed her hair.

"Then I think we should stay in Victoria and live in the apartment that Sharon found."

Rae wiped her eyes, looked up and tried to smile. "I guess you're stuck with me, then. I'll really try this time. A brand new start, all right?" She pulled Theo over to her and Theo let herself loosen inside her mother's arms.

22

"Make a wish, Theo!" cried Lisbeth.

Theo sat at the head of the Kaldors' dining-room table, a huge pink cake with ten candles on it in front of her. She closed her eyes.

I wish that there will be lots of other moments like this one, she thought. Then she blew out all the candles at once.

"Hurray!" Everyone clapped and Ben sang "Happy Birthday" again by himself.

"*Ten* ... double digits!" said Lisbeth with awe.

Theo lifted up the knife. "Don't cut all the way, it's bad luck," warned Anna. Sharon finished slicing the cake.

Theo swirled a delicious spoonful of peppermint sponge cake and strawberry ice cream in her mouth. She gazed down the table. Eleven other people were sitting at it, all here to celebrate *her* birthday! The six Kaldors, Rae and Sharon, and Skye, Robin and Carol. Each family had brought a dish for dinner and Sharon had made the beautiful cake.

Theo had worried about Rae meeting Laura and Dan, and Skye meeting their children—about mixing up all the people she knew in one house.

Sure enough, the first hour had been rocky. Dan looked uncomfortable as Carol ranted about how the university treated women. Theo watched Laura suppress her scorn at Rae's outfit—shocking pink bike shorts with a matching halter top. She saw how disapproving Dan and Laura looked when they sent John to find something to use as an ashtray.

When Skye began gushing over Lisbeth's Barbie collection, Anna said coolly, "You still play with Barbies? Even Lisbeth is tired of them." The Kaldors kept staring at Rae. They treated Theo gingerly, as if they had just met her.

But as the afternoon went on, Theo tried not to worry about how some of them rubbed against each other. Each of her family and friends was unique, that was all. Their discomfort wasn't *her* fault. She tried to distance herself, as Cecily had suggested. It wasn't easy, but it began to work a little. She became interested, instead of embarrassed, at observing everyone's interactions.

She couldn't remember ever having a real birthday party before. Some years Rae had bought a cake and candles; last year she'd forgotten completely. Theo tried not to think of that.

Today her mother had given her a white bathing suit covered with yellow flowers. "We'll go swimming this summer," she said. "I'll take you to Beaver Lake, where I used to go."

Sharon had bought Theo her first watch. Theo kept glancing at the important weight on her wrist. Skye had given her some barrettes with rainbow streamers on them. Robin and Carol had given her felt pens that changed colours. Ben drew her a picture of a dinosaur, Lisbeth and Anna had pooled their allowance to buy her a novel she'd wanted, and John had made her a flute out of a piece of bamboo.

The best present was from Laura and Dan—a painting Laura had done of all the Kaldors and Theo sitting on the steps of the house.

"Remember last month, when we went out to the front and Dan called that man coming up the street to take our picture?" said Laura. "I did it from that."

Theo remembered. It had been raining for days but then the sun had burst through the clouds and they'd gone out to breathe in the freshly washed air. It had been a shining moment.

She could hear Cecily's voice: "There are lots of shining moments." Now she had this picture to remind her of one of the many she'd shared with her favourite family. "*Thank* you," said Theo.

After they'd stuffed themselves with cake and ice cream, all six children left the adults and ran out to the cemetery.

"Are we allowed in here?" said Skye. "It's creepy!"

"We play here all the time," said Lisbeth. "Come on, let's race to the angel!" The others ran after her, John and Anna quickly taking the lead. Anna won, and dropped to the ground triumphantly.

"Is your mum a rock singer, Theo?" asked Lisbeth.

"Shut up, Lisbeth," hissed John.

"Why do you have two mummies, Skye?" said Ben.

Skye flushed.

"She just does, that's all," said Theo, giving her friend a reassuring smile.

"How do you like your new place?" Anna asked Theo.

"It's okay. There are two trees to climb and the dogs are really friendly."

"What kind are they?"

"Scotties. Scotch is old and fat, but Soda likes to chase sticks. Next week Mrs. Lundy's going away for three weeks and then we get to use the whole house." Theo paused. "You'll have to come over with Bingo. He'd like to play with the dogs."

"Sure!" said Anna.

Theo was relieved. Her new life still felt fragile; having the Kaldors over would make it more real.

Rae had found a job in a souvenir store on Government Street. She said it was easy: she spent all day talking to American tourists. When Theo got tired of hearing about them, she'd walk over to Sharon's and watch TV with her.

"Only a few more days of school," sighed Anna happily.

John looked anxious. "My last few days at this school," he reminded her.

"Don't worry, I bet you'll like grade eight," said Lisbeth. "You can go to dances and take out girls on dates." John looked even more worried.

"We're going camping for a week at Long Beach as soon as school's out," said Anna. "What are you doing, Skye?"

"I get to spend all summer with my father," said Skye eagerly. "He lives on a farm near Duncan. There's chickens and a donkey."

Anna looked at her with more respect. "I've never see a donkey," she said.

"How about you, Theo?" asked John.

"Rae can't take any holidays in the summer, but Sharon gets two weeks in August. She and I are going to stay at her friend Mandy's parents' place on Saltspring. Rae can come over on her days off."

"You'll like Saltspring," said Anna. "We camped there once."

"Could you come with us to Long Beach, Theo?" Lisbeth asked.

"We would have asked you before, but we weren't sure what your plans were," explained Anna.

Theo grinned at them. "I'll ask Rae," she said.

She curled her arms behind her neck and squinted at the sky. The summer had fallen into place, waiting for her to enjoy it. Everything would probably even happen the way it was arranged, she thought in wonder. And in the fall she'd go back to the same school again.

But would it stay the same? Maybe Rae would get restless. Maybe Sharon would finally travel.

If only kids were allowed to live alone—like Pippi Longstocking. I'd like to live in a tree, decided Theo. I'd cut shelves into the trunk for my dishes and food, and sleep on a hammock …

"What are you dreaming about, Theo?" asked Anna.

"She always does that," said Skye.

Theo smiled at her friends. She had them to turn to if things went wrong again. "Friends are like gold," Cecily had said.

She jumped up. "Let's play follow-the-leader!" She led them in a line through the cemetery. They skipped in and out of the shadows the thick foliage made on the grass. Theo held out one arm, walked with giant steps, hopped from leg to leg and waved her hands in the air.

She deliberately ended up at Cecily's grave, then took them in a dancing circle around it.

"*My* turn to be leader!" cried Lisbeth. "You have to go to the back of the line, Theo."

Theo ran behind Anna. Then she paused by the plot while the others dashed off.

She examined the white shrub rose Cecily had asked her to plant. Dan had helped her move it from the front garden of the house. They had clipped the grass and pulled up all the dandelions.

There was no sign of Cecily, of course. Theo knew she had gone away for good. She smoothed the marble pages of the book with her palms, as if she were pressing it firmly open.

"I won't forget," she whispered.

PUFFIN 🐧 CLASSICS

Awake and Dreaming

With Puffin Classics, the adventure isn't
over when you reach the final page.
Want to discover more about your favourite
characters, their creators, and their worlds?
Read on ...

CONTENTS

NAME: Kathleen Margaret Pearson
BORN: April 30, 1947
NATIONALITY: Canadian
LIVED: Edmonton, Alberta; Vancouver, British Columbia; St. Catharines, Ontario; Toronto, Ontario; now lives in Victoria, British Columbia
MARRIED: Common-law
CHILDREN: No

What is she like?

Kit is an optimistic and curious person whose mind is always preoccupied with the book she's writing and the book she's reading. When she's not writing or reading, she likes to garden, paint in watercolours, walk her dog, canoe at her cottage, and travel.

Where did she grow up and what was she like as a child?

Kit grew up with her two younger brothers in Edmonton, Alberta, and in Vancouver, British Columbia. She spent lots of time playing outdoors with various family dogs. An avid reader from a young age, she used books to fuel her imagination. She also escaped into reading because she was so shy. When she was older, she played many imaginary games with her two best friends. It was after reading L.M. Montgomery's *Emily of New Moon* at age twelve that Kit decided she wanted to be a writer. She studied English literature at the University of British Columbia and the University of Alberta, and got her masters of library science at the University of British Columbia.

What did she do apart from writing books?

She spent many years as a children's librarian, where she was surrounded by her favourite things: books! She could never get rid of the feeling that she was meant to be a writer herself. After taking a year off in Boston to study children's literature and writing, Kit decided to take the leap and wrote her first novel, *The Daring Game*.

Where did she get the idea for Awake and Dreaming?

Kit was inspired to write the novel when she overheard a conversation between a young girl and her mother on a ferry trip between Vancouver and Victoria, British Columbia. The girl had a look on her face that made Kit think that perhaps she was wishing for something, so Kit decided to write a story about Theo, a girl wishing for the perfect family. The setting for the novel is very true to life—you can even visit the cemetery in Victoria where the Kaldor children play.

What did people think of Awake and Dreaming when it was first published?

The novel was very well received when it was published, and it went on to be translated into Japanese, Chinese, and Korean. The book won multiple awards in Canada, including the highly regarded Governor General's Award.

What other books did she write?

Kit has written ten novels, including *A Handful of Time, Looking at the Moon*, and *A Perfect Gentle Knight*, as well as a picture book titled *The Singing Basket*. Her short stories have appeared in multiple collections. Her most recent novel is *And Nothing But the Truth*.

Theo Caffrey – Nine-year-old Theo lives with her unreliable mother, Rae. Theo is constantly moving from school to school when her mother loses her job or when they need to change apartments. She loves books and uses them as a way to escape her real life.

Rae Caffrey – Theo's twenty-five-year-old mother. Rae has trouble holding down a job, and finds it difficult to get enough money to pay the rent and to keep food on the table.

Sharon Caffrey – Rae's sister and Theo's aunt who agrees to take Theo into her home, providing stability and consistency for the first time in Theo's life.

Cal – Rae's boyfriend, who isn't sure if he likes children very much.

John Kaldor – John is the eldest of the Kaldor children. He enjoys playing piano, and in Theo's dream world he teaches Theo how to ride a bike.

Anna Kaldor – At ten years old, Anna loves to play soccer and ride her bike.

Lisbeth Kaldor – Lisbeth is seven, and is lively and a bit spoiled.

Ben Kaldor – the youngest Kaldor child at age four.

Laura Rice – Laura is the mother of the Kaldor children and a talented graphic artist.

Dan Kaldor – Dan is the father of the Kaldor children and teaches English at the University of Victoria. He has a huge book collection, of which he is very proud.

Mr. Barker – the teacher who encourages Theo's writing when he hears her poetry in class.

Mrs. Mitic – a neighbour in Theo's apartment building. She occasionally looks in on Theo when Rae is out late or is away for a weekend.

Ms. Sunter – the school counsellor who helps get Theo some second-hand clothes. She tells Theo that just because she's poor, it doesn't mean she can't be successful in life.

Ms. Tremblay – Theo's dream-world teacher.

Grace Leung – Anna's best friend.

Skye – Theo's friend who is also new to the school. She wants Theo to be her best friend.

Robin – Skye's mother, a nurse.

Carol – Robin's partner, who works as a freelance writer.

Cecily Stone – an author who died forty years ago. Theo meets her in the cemetery near the Kaldor house.

Theo has changed schools more than five times. What do you think it would feel like to always be the "new kid"? How can you help a new classmate fit in?

Theo uses books in order to escape from the troubles of her daily life. What do you do or where do you go if you feel the need to escape?

Were you surprised at how Rae treated Theo? Do you think Theo felt unloved at the beginning of the novel? Do you feel that that changed by the end?

In Theo's dream, she fits in perfectly with the Kaldor family, but in reality they have conflicts like everyone else. Do you think there is such a thing as the perfect family?

On page 40, Theo feels that it's safe to be invisible. What do you think she means by this?

Sharon tries her best to make Theo comfortable in her home, but Theo doesn't respond to her. Do you think Theo acts fairly toward Sharon?

Before Cecily leaves Theo at the end of the novel, she suggests that perhaps Theo could write a story about the difficult life she has had. Do you think Theo will eventually write that story? Why or why not?

Theo has read a lot of books in her nine years. Can you remember all the books you've read? Keep a book journal in which you can record the title of each book, the author, and what you thought of it. It's a great way to remember your reading history.

Investigate if there are any authors that came from your own community, like Cecily Stone. Find out the titles of their books and where you can find copies. Do the authors use your community as a backdrop for their stories?

Write a short story about a "perfect family." What would that family be like and what sort of activities would they do together?

Mr. Barker asked his class to write a poem using the lines he wrote on the board. Try doing the same thing and see what you come up with:

What is pink? (or choose some other colour) *What is peace? What is love? What is friendship? What is happiness?*

Much of this story takes place in the Ross Bay Cemetery in Victoria. If you live in or near Victoria, visit it and try to find the graves that are mentioned in the book. You can also go on a cemetery tour with Kit every year; see her website for the upcoming date. Or visit a cemetery in your own city or town. What stories do the gravestones tell?

In her story, Kit Pearson used other locations within Victoria as well. When you look around your neighbourhood, what areas would be good settings for a work of fiction?

BOOKS WITHIN THE BOOK

There are numerous mentions of other books within this novel; some of them you may recognize and some you may not. Here are just a few of the books Theo has read. Maybe you could read them, too!

All-of-a-Kind Family by Sydney Taylor – Five sisters love doing everything together and turn everyday tasks into an adventure.

Ballet Shoes by Noel Streatfeild – The story of three orphan girls who are growing up together in unusual circumstances and are sent to dance school.

Charlotte's Web by E.B. White – A beautiful tale of friendship between Wilbur, the pig, and a spider named Charlotte.

The Family from One End of the Street by Eve Garnett – Follow the antics of the Ruggles family who are always on the lookout for fun.

Five Children and It by E. Nesbit – While digging in the sand, five children uncover a sand fairy who grants them a wish every day, often with unexpected results.

Half Magic by Edward Eager – Three sisters and their brother find a magical coin that grants half wishes.

Little Women by Louisa May Alcott – With their father away at war, the March sisters endure hardships but also share their joy in this classic novel.

The Moffats by Eleanor Estes – The Moffat family find themselves in mischief on a daily basis in small-town Connecticut.

The Princess and the Goblin by George MacDonald – Princess Irene discovers a secret stairway in a castle that leads to a maze of stairways, doors, and most important, adventure.

Swallows and Amazons by Arthur Ransome – The Walker children enjoy a summer of epic battles on their boat, the *Swallow*.

Thumbelina by Hans Christian Andersen – No bigger than your thumb, tiny Thumbelina is kidnapped by a toad and must use her quick thinking to escape.